Onlyville

❀

ONLYVILLE

Cynthia Holz

with engravings by G. Brender à Brandis

The Porcupine's Quill, Inc.

CANADIAN CATALOGUING IN PUBLICATION DATA

Holz, Cynthia, 1950-
Onlyville

ISBN 0-88984-178-0

I. Title.

PS8565.O5905 1994   C813'.54   C94-930425-5
PR9199.3.H605 1994

Published by The Porcupine's Quill, Inc.,
68 Main Street, Erin, Ontario NOB 1TO
with financial assistance from
The Canada Council and the Ontario Arts Council.
The support of the Government of Ontario
through the Ministry of Culture, Tourism and Recreation
is also gratefully acknowledged.

The author also thanks
The Canada Council and the Toronto Arts Council
for their generous assistance.

Represented in Canada by the Literary Press Group.
Trade orders available from General Distribution Services
in Canada (Toronto) and the United States (Niagara Falls).
Selected titles also available from Inland Book Company.

Readied for the press by John Metcalf.
Copy edited by Doris Cowan.

Cover is after a photograph by S. Cohen/Comstock.

For Deborah Levine

PART ONE

ONE: 1974

THE *Island Queen* moves slowly, creaking and rolling on the bay like a porch rocker caught in a breeze. Standing in the bow I can smell rot and lacquer; I can see the island in the distance, balanced on the horizon.

The boat sounds its whistle as it arcs through the channel to Onlyville. After it docks I climb off, my legs unsteady and slow. Under my feet the pier shifts as the boat bumps the boards and they rise a bit, then flatten out. The pier is nearly empty. In August people come in droves, you can hardly make your way from the dock to the main street. But this is April, off-season, no one to collide with. I swing my duffel bag over my shoulder and head off.

Near the dock the General Store is now Jack's Mini-Mart. Next to that is something new, a restaurant and bar called the Sea Breeze. On The Boulevard the bungalows that line the street are mostly unchanged. Some have new windows and doors but all are still bleached white, their roofs shades of faded blue. At the end of the street I turn onto Atlantic Walk, the ocean running next to me. The wind blows it into my face – a briny smell, that crashing – and I quicken my step.

Then the cottage is just ahead, wet-looking, crooked, with a sagging deck. The front yard a patch of sand with an old cedar and clumps of grass. I shove my hand in my jeans pocket, feeling for keys. Two sets of keys in there, one to the cottage, one to Sal's apartment. That's when my thoughts change course and I start thinking of Sal again, the person I most want to forget. Wondering if he's read my note, if he'll try and find me anyway. Is he already on his way here? I bang my head with the heel of my hand because I don't want to think like that.

I open the door and step inside. My nose wrinkles up at the mustiness and my arms rise, fighting off imaginary cobwebs. I heave my sack onto a chair and look around. Behind me, on the west wall, the framed map my father bought and hung in 1951, a map of the island simply drawn with gray dots for cottages and broken lines to indicate the ferry routes. Next to that the grandfather clock that hasn't worked in twenty years. I run my fingers over the case carefully, like reading braille.

In the living room the furniture has been rearranged. I cough dust as I move things around, back to where they used to be, then find a rag and wipe the rocker, tables and chairs. In the guest room some uncle or aunt has left a vase in the shape of a barn, which I hide under the stairwell. There are figurines on the kitchen counter, pig-tailed girls and boys in breeches, a miniature herd of cows and goats. I stash the collection in a box and shove it to the back of a cupboard, catching a whiff of sourness that might be some last trace of breath mints or tobacco.

Upstairs the bedroom windows are jammed shut, some of the panes cracked through. There are brown stains on the ceilings where the roof leaked. Everyone's been after me to sell while the house is still standing, but I won't. This is the only place I know to go where I can feel safe.

I unpack my duffel bag downstairs in the guest room and make the bed with clean sheets. The ceiling's dry here and the windows work; I open them wide. Then I head for the patio doors and step out on the sundeck. Light rain is falling as I lean against the deck rail and stare at the scene before me, scrub and grass, sand and sea, everything gray and misty. I picture myself in a thin gown, my silhouette showing through as I walk in fog along the shore: cool and mysterious, the kind of woman I want to be.

My sewing machine and boxes are arriving on the evening boat. I need something to load them on, a wagon like the one I saw alongside the Mini-Mart. I didn't like the look of the place with its new enlarged sign, but I walk back and go inside. The store carries frozen foods, packaged meats and canned goods, all of it expensive. No licorice or yo-yo's or thirty-five-cent paperbacks, no shovels, pails and coloring books. I can't help feeling let down.

A fan turns overhead but the air is stale. In the vegetable aisle a young man in green fatigues is building a pyramid of plastic-wrapped zucchini. I fill a wire basket and put it on the counter; finally he wipes his hands and goes behind the register.

'My brother used to work here when Mr. Wagner owned the store. Jay Berman?'

No reply. His fingers tap the register keys and he keeps his eyes fixed on his hand.

'I guess you wouldn't know him, it was years ago.'

He looks at me sidelong, his eyes of no particular color, as if they've been drawn with a pencil. 'Nineteen fifty-four,' he says.

'It was '58.'

He bangs the register drawer open – 'I'm talking about your groceries' – and I whip a twenty out of my pocket and slap it down. He takes the bill, makes change and bags the food.

'Listen,' I say with false cheeriness, 'mind if I use that wagon at the side of the store? I've got some boxes coming on the next boat.'

He turns to stare out the window, at the plate glass dark with drizzle.

'Because it's raining,' I try again. 'Because I don't want to carry boxes in the rain. I'll bring it right back.' But already I'm thinking, Just forget it, carry the boxes in the rain and don't go begging this creep for help.

He swings his head around. 'Take it, I don't care.' Then he leaves the register and goes back to his green zucchini pyramid.

I grab my bags and dash out, glancing over my shoulder as I hurry back to the cottage. Once inside I get the feeling I've left something at the store. I put the bags on the kitchen table and empty them out. Nothing missing. I count the change in my jeans pocket: all there. A shadow scoots across the floor and I cry out.

It's raining hard when I go to meet the five o'clock boat. My shoes slap the boardwalk and water wriggles down my neck. The ferry crew unloads my portable sewing machine, the boxes of cloth and other stuff, but the Mini-Mart is closed by then, the wagon gone. No one's around so I carry what I can myself, one box, then another, then the Singer so heavy I have to stop and rest every few feet. Finally it's done and I'm back in the cottage, wet and cold, surrounded by my soggy gear.

I head for the old rocker in the living room. I want to flop down in it but then I don't, remembering that one of its rear legs is cracked – although unless you knew where to look you'd never know it was broken. When I was a girl I would forget, I'd fall into the chair and suddenly wind up twisted, my right side thrown back. Now I sit down carefully and rest my hands on the rocker's arms, as smooth and cool as always. I want to rock but of course I can't, so I sit still and concentrate on the feel of the wood. Then I'm thinking of driftwood, walking sticks and boardwalks, red wagons, wooden toys. And it's like I'm sailing to somewhere else, to long ago when I was a cop and Jay a robber, I was Daddy's Honeybear and summer was the shortest, sweetest season of all.

I've come with a plan, to start my own business. No more office temp jobs, though I can type a hundred and ten words a minute without paying attention. No one here to interrupt so I'll work hard, sewing a line of one-of-a-kind denim clothes for children. Jeans and jackets, skirts, jumpers, vests and accessories, everything studded, starred, quilted, appliquéd. I'll sew like mad till the end of June and sell what I can to the summer crowd. Someday I'll open a small boutique in the Cove.

At night, unable to sleep, I try to think about my plan and how to order the days ahead. I lie in bed and concentrate, but the dark is alive with a thousand sounds – blowing sand, clamoring surf, the wind and the complaints of the house. Panes rattle, hinges squeak, and I picture people running to escape the house or circling it, trying to find a way in. Hearing their breath, feeling it hot and sticky on my forehead, I go stiff and want to cry. But don't cry. I almost never cry anymore.

When I can't stand it any longer I get out of bed and turn on every light upstairs. Then I do the same thing downstairs. The light helps. I lie on the couch in the living room and wait for dawn. When the windows brighten and birds scratch in the eavestroughs I fall asleep.

The sun is high when I jerk awake, crying 'Sal!' Then I remember where I am. I make coffee and drink it on the sundeck. You can see the beach clearly from there, a bright blade of white sand. Farther out, waves rising and falling. On the bay side a ferry blows its whistle and a motor boat revs up, whining like a buzz saw. Someone is hammering nearby, someone else beating a rug. I feel the island's strong pulse and am eager to get to work.

I cut, pin, baste, stitch, and the chugging of the Singer joins the island hum in a driving song. I imagine pieces matching up and racks of clothing filling up, can see every brick and hook and hanger of my Cove boutique. Which makes me sew even faster, and faster still.

I don't stop till I'm famished, then eat something from a can. The sun has already gone down and the house is strange with shadows. Onlyville is silent again, like a switch has been thrown. In the quiet I remember noise, the two years I lived with Sal, the radio playing constantly because he's a journalist and nothing excites him more than news. It got so I'd hardly hear it at all; I'd get my news from the papers. Now I wish I'd brought along a radio. Another voice would be nice here.

I wander around the living room. There are moldy-smelling novels in the bookcase, faded women's magazines, a stack of *Reader's Digest*s and some taped-together children's books. I know them all, can track my life from Disney classics to 'Humor in Uniform,' on to the secrets of makeup and coordinates as told in *Vogue,* and finally to Mother's favorite love story, *A Farewell to Arms.* I touch the spine but leave the book, I don't want to read. Instead I play a record on the phonograph.

South Pacific. Which ought to put me in some dreamy island mood but only makes me think of Sal. Again Sal. That downtown party: Sal across a crowded room. The air conditioner sputtered and the drone of traffic outside was steady and loud, but above it all I heard him laugh, his deep and hearty laughter. It buzzed through me, put an extra beat in my pulse, and I elbowed across the room. His voice sure and rich as he ticked off Nixon's failings to a circle of guests. I slipped in beside him. I didn't like the look of him much up close, his mutton chops and slightly unfocused stare, but my knees bumped together when he roared with assertiveness, 'The Pentagon Papers prove the rot in this administration!' Later –

we were all stoned – he rolled up his sleeves, switched on a radio and asked me to dance. I tripped into his long arms and spread into that hollow space like water fills a container. I came up to his collarbone and his chin rested heavily on top of my head. I thought, *Now I've found him*. I thought, *Never let him go*.

This isn't helping one bit.

❀

By the end of a week I've developed a habit of sleepless nights, lost mornings, busy afternoons and restless evenings. I've begun taking walks on the beach, once before lunch, once after supper, hunting for shells and colored stones and beach glass. Whatever I find goes into a clear bowl on the kitchen counter, something added every time, the arrangement changing daily as the hill rises inch by inch. My calendar. Every day I get through is a day farther away from Sal.

On Sunday I go for an outing. I pack a lunch, a sketch pad and book and head for the old lighthouse, walking southeast along the shore. In a couple of hours the lantern of the lighthouse rises slowly from behind the dunes. I start hurrying, seeing pictures in my head: the peaked roof of the keeper's house, his small yard and white gate, stairs to the top of the tower and the great lamp. I remember the old keeper pointing, 'Look over there,' and how I'd follow his finger to a tiny ship far below. It was like he'd shared a secret with me, and I was too astounded to speak.

But when I actually get there the keeper's house is boarded up, the lighthouse door chained shut. I throw stones at shuttered windows, slow at first but then fast. I think I hear glass breaking and that makes me aim better, throw harder than before. I want the whole house to shatter – first the windows, then the walls! – but the house survives my hail of rocks and finally I'm tired out. I drag my feet through sand as I backtrack across the beach and sink to my knees close to shore. Overhead the sky has turned cloudy and gray, and the sand that rubs against my legs is rough with butts and plastic straws. I eat lunch in the middle of this. I skim a chapter of *Islands of the Atlantic*. Then I take the pad and pencil from my bag and draw some lines on a clean sheet. It isn't the lighthouse that I sketch but a lifeguard's chair, face down, partly buried in the sand. Like the skeleton of a lost bird that died in this lonely place.

By the second week I can sleep at night, the darkness is familiar, my breathing part of the conversations of the night, the whispering and grumbling like the talk of women over tea. I sleep eleven hours a night, don't remember my dreams and don't want to. I wake at nine, walk on the beach, eat something and face the day's pile of cloth. I'm spending more time away from the Singer doing hand work, cutting and quilting hearts and flowers, trimming with beads and French knots, writing 'Love' and 'Peace Now' in a chain stitch. Sewing mornings and afternoons but nothing seems to get done, there's always something more to add, another star, another moon. Layer after layer of embroidery and appliqué, clothing with the heaviness of wall hangings. While I feel lighter and lighter, insubstantial.

One afternoon I stop sewing and look in a mirror. I see someone ghostly, her hair falling in tangled roots. Then I feel a breath on my neck just at the seam where my hair parts and drops forward. Turning fast I see nothing. 'Who's there?' I cry out. From nearby I hear a sound – a snap or crack. I rush to a window and catch a glimpse of something – someone? – skittering off. I turn to the mirror again, afraid of what I'll see in the glass. I see my chest rising and falling, one-two, one-two. My pulse is beating in my ears.

The level of stones in the bowl on the counter rises again: my third week in Onlyville. Now my head feels overfull, so heavy on my neck that I move slowly, sew little, want to nap. But don't nap. Nights are for sleeping, days are not. I force myself to walk on the beach and sketch what I notice on those walks, my drawings as true as photographs – starfish and jellyfish washed ashore, plants and dunes and animal bones. By now the sun is stronger, I can go barefoot on the beach and the sand warms the soles of my feet. Ferry service has increased and all at once there are more people milling about. Someone is always out with his dog, couples jog and threesomes toss a football. I call out to whoever I see, careful to keep my voice light: 'Nice morning!' 'Good throw!' Like learning to talk all over again, the words sticky on my tongue. People wave and shout hello, but no one stops.

In the Mini-Mart the stock has grown and the boy in green fatigues isn't alone anymore. An old man stands by the checkout, ringing up groceries. I think they must be father and son although they don't look much alike and nothing in their behavior signals closeness.

At the checkout I lift my basket, and the old man starts to talk. 'You're up early,' he says. 'Not hung over, I hope.' He winks at me. 'Where you staying?'

'On Blueberry. The house on the dunes.'

'Don't know it. Never mind. Every time you look there's another cottage going up and new people moving in.' He starts whistling, something that sounds like the national anthem, his fingers keeping time on the register keys.

'Maybe you knew Mr. Wagner,' I say. 'He owned the General Store several years ago.'

'This store? Angus Henry sold it to me . . . never heard of Wagner. That's the way it is today, buy and sell, move on. So many new houses, so many new names you can't keep up.'

'Ours is an old house, it's been here forever. The Berman place.'

He frowns. 'You're staying there alone?'

'Why shouldn't I?'

He shakes his head. 'A young lady, an empty house . . .' Then he turns away and starts whistling that anthem-song again.

After that I stay close to the cottage. Instead of walking along the shore I pace the deck. With nothing to add to the bowl of shells I lose track of the days of the week. Now there are only days and nights and even these run together. I feel sleepy all the time and don't care. I nap when the sun is high or low, it doesn't matter. I play the same records over and over on the phonograph, an old recording of *Porgy and Bess* or *Showboat*.

One day when a record is on, turned up loud, I start to dance, slide-stepping, spinning in circles, arms bent like I'm holding a partner. I never hear the sound of footsteps on the deck, the sucking noise as the door opens, but sense someone in the room. I stop cold, my back to whoever it is, frozen in my ridiculous pose.

'Summertime' is playing on the phonograph.

When I turn around and see Sal, I catch my breath. 'Baby,' he says as he ties his arms around me, 'you knew I'd find you, didn't you?'

❀

Sal has a manual typewriter, a suitcase and a radio. 'Didn't think you'd have electricity,' he says as he lays the typewriter on the table opposite my Singer. He puts the radio on the fridge and flicks it on.

Something clicks awake in me. 'What're you doing?'

'Setting up shop. I took a six-month leave and I'm going to write a book.'

'What?'

'Nothing like what I do for the magazine, no financial advice stuff. This'll be a bestseller, wheeling and dealing, murder, drugs, the whole shebang.'

'You can't stay,' I tell him.

His jaw drops and he rubs the side of his face like it's hurting. Then he walks up to me and cups my face in his big hands. 'Look, I know I haven't been paying attention to you. You know how hard it's been at work ... but that's all behind us now. We can be together all day, every day, real close. I'll write this book and you,' he pauses, 'you can do whatever you want. What do you say?'

I like the feel of his hands on my face, so I stand there and let him hold me awhile. Then I wiggle out of his grip. 'I want to be alone. I don't want you here.'

'You've been alone four weeks and look at you, you look like a ghost. When was the last time you washed your hair, huh? Seems to me you need some looking after. Thank your lucky stars I went and tracked you down. I had to call your brother long-distance too and he wasn't even sure you'd be here.'

'Go,' I say, 'I'm okay.' Something wobbly in my voice.

He circles the kitchen and living room and pokes his head in the guest room. He climbs the stairs and glances around, then clumps down. 'Better than I expected, not too primitive.' He comes up behind me and kisses me on the back of the neck. I make a sound in my throat – it just comes out of me.

'Let me stay?'

I can't speak.

He swings me around and dabs my face with tiny kisses. 'Anna, I missed you, couldn't stand it. Don't ever do that to me again, just disappear. I was worried sick.'

I try to speak but he puts a finger on my lips and shushes me. Then he gets a paper towel and dusts the table and kitchen chairs. He sweeps the floors and swats cobwebs off the walls. He scrubs the sink and brushes the bathroom bowl clean. I follow him from room to room, my cheeks getting hot. By the time he starts defrosting the fridge my fingers are itching for something to do.

He examines the shelves. 'There's nothing here to eat. What are you living on?'

'I'm on a budget,' I explain.

'You're not eating enough. Look how skinny you are.' He draws a wad of bills from his pocket and holds them out. 'Here, take it. Stock the cupboards, fill the fridge. Buy enough for both of us.'

'I don't want your money.'

'Here we go again. No one's allowed to help you.'

'It's not no one we're talking about. It's you – I don't want *you* to help.'

'Don't get so excited,' he says. He tucks the bills away and raises a hand. 'I'll be right back.' Then he leaves through the patio door.

He comes back a while later carrying a box of groceries and empties the box on the table. Out come expensive things like steaks and wine and cold cuts. Fresh fruit. Vanilla fudge ice cream.

'I don't want you to do this, Sal.'

'Why don't you sit outside on the chaise and I'll bring you a beer.'

'I don't want a beer.'

'Ice cream?'

'I want you to take this stuff back.'

'Don't be silly. I'm not going to starve even if you are. Now if you'll get out of my way I'll start supper. Pork chops *alla Modenese*. How's that?'

I go out on the deck and collapse in the chaise. The smell of frying meat blows through the window screen and my mouth waters, my stomach talks. But I won't eat his cooking. Not a damn thing. One bite and I'm done for: the next would go down easier. I know how easy it is to lose yourself in pieces, bit by bit.

Sal brings out a plate of antipasto and puts it on a low table next to the chaise. 'I thought you might be hungry.'

'I'm not, so you can take it away.'

'Maybe later.' He leaves the plate and goes in.

Then I don't see him again for an hour. My stomach's really howling by then. I could go inside and make a sandwich but don't want to deal with Sal yet and don't want to see those pork chops. Anyway, I'm comfortable here. Why not relax and enjoy this? Have a mushroom, have an olive. What harm can one lousy olive do?

Or a celery stick.

A plum tomato.

Mortadella sausage.

Better to deal with Sal on a full stomach, I decide.

He brings me a glass of wine. Cold, with a slight furry taste. He goes back and forth, keeping my glass full.

The pork chops are delicious.

After dinner he carries me into one of the bedrooms upstairs. I think of Clark Gable carrying Vivien Leigh in *Gone with the Wind*, which makes me wet between the legs. In bed my mind is numb but my body works; it knows exactly how to move. It does what it does so well that Sal is tricked into thinking all is fine again. I hear his voice from miles away. I hear him say, 'We'll be together always.' Right before I fall asleep I hear a shrill *no!* in my head. Then it fades and I curl up against his back.

In the morning, first thing, he turns up the radio. From where I lie upstairs I hear clearly a solemn voice: '. . . would not reveal the whole truth to government investigators, or so the tapes indicate.'

The word *tape* plays in my head: Scotch tape, masking tape, tape recorder, ticker tape, tape deck, tape measure, tapeworm, tapering. I roll over, pulling the bedclothes over my face. The sheets give off the smell of sex and mustiness. I shrink under the covers but the radio gets louder. Sal comes into the room and yanks the sheets down, exposing my head.

'Rise and shine!' He licks my ear and I shudder. He's carrying the radio in one hand, a hammer and chisel in the other. I sit up and yawn.

'Sssh!' he says.

'". . . try to cut our losses . . ."'

'Listen to this, it's from the edited transcripts.'

'". . . a million dollars to take care of the jackasses who are in jail. That can be arranged. That could be arranged . . ."'

'They're going to nail the sonuvabitch!' Sal says. His ears are turning crimson.

I blink at him. 'Who?'

'*Who*, she says. Don't you read the papers, don't you care what's going on out there?' He swings his arm at the window overlooking the sea as if whatever's going on is happening in the Atlantic. 'The President of the United States is about to get his head axed and you don't know who I'm talking about.'

'I do,' I answer sheepishly. 'Richard Milhous Nixon.'

'Anna, this is big stuff. Watergate is big news. I know you're only twenty-nine but you should care about these things. What happens on the Hill will affect your life!'

I inch out of bed, stark naked, wishing I had something on. I fold an arm across my breasts and drop a hand over my crotch. 'I do care.'

From the radio: '". . . prick the boil and take the heat . . ."'

Sal turns the volume up and puts the radio on the floor, then starts prying the window with his chisel. 'We need some air in here!' he shouts over the noise.

I get dressed and go downstairs. In the kitchen I sit at the counter drinking black coffee, trying to jolt myself awake. Sal comes down in a little while, the radio in his hand again but turned down to medium low. He looks at me and shakes his head, 'You need a big breakfast,' then turns and busies himself at the stove. I hear him cracking eggs and hear the eggs spattering in a pan. Then he rushes outside and comes back with a handful of twigs. Forsythia. I never noticed them growing on the island before. He sticks them in an empty bottle and puts the bottle in front of the counter window. It looks just right there, a yellow spray against the blues and spring greens beyond the glass.

Sal brings me a plate of eggs over easy, the way I like them, whole wheat toast and sliced tomatoes drizzled with oil. I stare at the food and can't decide if I'm hungry or not. I lift my fork, put it down. Lift it again.

'Irresistible,' Sal says.

Does he mean me?

He sits down on the next stool and drops his arm across my shoulders, closing it around my neck. 'Mind if I watch you eat?'

❀

I can't think with Sal in the house, there's too much noise. Not just the radio going day and night but the clackety-clack of the typewriter keys, the thud of his step, the roll of his voice as he paces the rooms muttering. He interrupts me whenever he likes. 'How's this?' and he'll read some lines from his manuscript: 'She had the ripe blond looks of Cybill Shepherd. Her breasts were like apples and her beautiful ass was shaped like a pear. But this was no lady, Cage reminded himself. This was a killer.'

'Sounds like she belongs in a fruit bowl.'

Sal puts down the page and frowns. 'Don't joke about my book. I want your considered opinion.'

I'm stem-stitching a target and bull's-eye onto the back of a jacket and I don't look up, but my needle stops. 'Maybe you should write it first, the whole thing. Then we'll talk.'

He flips his wrist at my suggestion. 'What's the point of finishing a lousy book?'

'I didn't say it was lousy.'

'You didn't exactly jump for joy.'

'Well, I think you've got to work on character. That doesn't mean...'

But Sal has already torn the page and stomped out. I brush my sewing off my lap and run to a window, watching as he disappears behind a dune. Moments later I see him in the distance, a flash at the water's edge. I turn off the radio, hurry to the guest room and fall on the bed, listening to the sudden calm, watching the light in the curtains. After a while my eyes hurt and I close them. I hear gurgling in my ears and feel pressure in my chest, as if I'm slowly filling up with water.

When Sal wakes me the room is full of shadows. He sits on the bed with his head ducked and speaks in a low voice. 'I shouldn't be writing crap,' he says. 'I should be writing a book like Woodward and Bernstein's.'

I put a hand on his shoulder. 'You're not that kind of reporter, Sal.'

His eyes are downcast. 'Well, I could be.'

I turn him around and pull his head against my breast. His face, like a slab of wax, molds to my flesh. 'Yes you could,' I say. 'You can be anything you want to be.'

We sleep right there on the narrow bed in the guest room. Hours later I wake again to the sound of Sal grinding his teeth. I slip out from under his arm and cross the room. 'Die, bastard, die!' he groans. The mattress creaks and I know he's thrashing back and forth though I can't see him in the dark. The first time it frightened me to hear him calling out like that, to see him writhing in his sleep, but soon enough I was used to it: Sal's dream. Night after night he'd fight and strangle a North Korean sniper with his bare hands.

The Korean War. My God. He seems so old to me sometimes.

I step to the bed and shine a flashlight over him. The mutton chops and moustache give him a military look, but a curl twisting over his ear reminds me of the boy behind the whiskers. I kiss his forehead, feeling the wet heat of his skin against my lips. 'Die!' he gasps. Then he starts whimpering, caught in the pain of his dream.

The room is stuffy, I need air. I go outside and spread my arms. My chest hurts when I breathe in. A damp breeze shakes my hair, fills and ruffles my nightgown. The surf is close. It sounds like it's rolling up to the house and reaching for my ankles. I breathe out slowly. He has to go, I tell myself. The only way.

Lights are on when I go inside, a tap running. Sal comes out of the bathroom and downstairs, his face puffy, dripping water.

'You okay?'

He shakes his head. His eyes are pink at the edges.

'You were dreaming again.' I lead him back to the guest room and hold his hand till he falls asleep. I'll tell him in the morning when he's rested.

Sal is up before me, I can hear him in the kitchen, but I won't eat anything. I'll get right to the point – *Sal, you have to go.*

But I love you, he'll say.

I need space.

You need me.

That's when I'll get tough: *Sal, get out my house.*

You can't mean it. After all I've done for you . . .

My stomach's tight as I pause by the fridge to hear a woman's choked voice on the radio: 'I voted for him, believed in him. Now I don't know what to think.'

Sal sees me standing there. He hands me coffee and waves me onto a kitchen stool. 'Let's get out of the house,' he says. 'I'll buy you brunch. Where can we find a restaurant?'

My mouth falls open. Brunch? I don't want brunch. I don't want him doing anything nice for me.

'What's open around here?'

'Nothing,' I say.

'So what about another town?' He walks up to the map on the wall. 'This one here – the Cove – looks like a big place. We'll try that.' Then he strides into the kitchen. 'How fast can you get ready?'

I'm sitting in a black kimono, trying to get my coffee down. I swallow hard. 'Listen, Sal . . .'

He yanks the radio off the fridge and hurries out the door, calling, 'Meet you on the corner.'

I leave the coffee and go upstairs. I get dressed, fumbling my clothes, and pull on a hat. Lunch in a quiet restaurant with a view of the bay . . . that's when I'll tell him to clear out.

We walk inland, away from the beach, the most direct path to the Cove. The radio swings between us, and I hear bits of an interview. 'The pulse quickens,' a woman says, '. . . engorged with blood.' Sal is breathing hard, taking long strides. I think of our first night in bed, his eyes sliding over me, his heavy breathing overhead. And I felt I was running toward it, chasing the sound, that my life depended on reaching it, I had to run as fast as I could – faster still! – to catch his breath. His breath racing in my ears.

'A satisfying climax,' the radio says.

At last the Cove is just ahead, a crescent of cottages facing the bay. Sal follows me past the church and tennis courts to Bayside, a street of shops with kegs of flowers and potted cedars out front. People gaze at store windows or stand chattering on the walk. Nearby, from the northerly direction of the Island Bridge, a car sputters, a horn beeps. 'This is more like it,' Sal says, 'a real place.'

We stop to eat at Jolly Roger's and find seats by a window overlooking the bay. Sal turns the radio down and sets it on the floor at his feet. A waiter appears, a patch over his left eye, and tells us we're too late for brunch.

'Just as well,' Sal says. He orders steak and wine. 'Put some color back in your cheeks.'

'But I'd rather have fish.'

'Trust me.'

I frown and turn to look at the bay, rippled with swells and whitecaps. A ferry hoots again and again. A sailboat bobs in the distance and my stomach drops.

Sal is talking quickly now, his voice grave. Somehow I've missed the moment when the conversation heated up. 'Do you?' he says. 'Believe in me?'

I don't answer.

'Because if you do, I really think I can write a book, a good book, something you'd be proud of. A serious one about the war. Korea. But if you don't believe in me . . . ' His voice fades.

The waiter pours our wine and I drink quickly. Sal watches me steadily. 'Slow down,' he warns.

I feel my head spiraling when I speak again. 'Why don't we ever talk about what I want to do, my work?'

His eyebrows peak. 'Office temp?'

'Sewing, I mean. You see those little shops out there?' I wag a finger at the door and the street beyond. 'I want one of those, my own children's wear boutique, geraniums in a window box and everything.'

'Sewing?' he says. 'I can't keep up with you. Yoga, drawing, now this.'

'I mean it, Sal, I'm serious.'

He leans across the table, coming up close. 'Whether you believe in me or not, I believe in you, honest to God. You want to run a store, I'm with you all the way. No matter what.'

I empty another glass of wine. 'The point is . . . I can't get any sewing done with you around. You take up too damn much space. The house is always full of noise –'

'The house!' he interrupts, 'that's the problem. That place is really creepy, you know. I think it must be haunted or something, I hear these footsteps late at night. Impossible to concentrate, I know what you mean.' He draws my hands to his mouth and kisses the knuckles. 'Let's move – we'll move to the Cove. You do the store and I'll write.'

'It's *you* I'm talking about – there's nothing wrong with the house!'

He drops my hands. 'I don't see why you need quiet just to sew but if that's what you want, fine, I'll try to be quieter. Okay?'

Our food arrives but we don't eat. 'Sal,' I say, 'this is the second time I've left. It didn't work in the city and it won't work here.'

He lowers his head. 'I can't believe I'm hearing this. You must be drunk.'

'I'm not drunk.'

'We've been together all this time, you just don't want to throw that away.'

'Two years is not so long.'

He shoves his plate aside and hunches forward. I feel his hot breath on my face. 'I'm everything to you, Anna – mother, father, lover, friend. No one cares about you like I do, nobody.

Understand? It's a big lousy world out there, you'll never make it on your own.'

My throat is closing up but I say the words, 'I can't live with you, I can't. I tried and I can't.'

He reaches down and turns off the radio. 'I love you, Anna. The real thing.'

I push away from the table and stagger outside. On the street I fall against the shingled wall of the restaurant and sink to a squat, wheezing for air. Someone comes up beside me: 'Excuse me, are you all right?'

I nod, squeezing my eyes shut, and pull my hat low on my face. Then I hear a haughty voice, 'I'll take care of her, she's with me.' An arm slips around my back and Sal lifts me gently, gently, upright. My feet are spongy on the ground. I have to watch them closely to be sure they're moving properly, one in front of the other. Sal hooks me into a space between his chest and upper arm and half carries me down the walk. The radio is playing again. A man says in formal tones, '. . . and God bless each and every one of you.'

I'm tired after the trek back. All I want to do is sleep, but when we're in sight of the house my back stiffens, my knees lock. Something's wrong. Sal tugs my arm, 'Come on, we're almost there.'

'Wait a minute – let go! I think someone's in the house.'

'A burglar? How would you know from here?'

'I feel it.'

He runs off and comes back with a piece of wood shaped like a club. 'Okay, we'll check it out.'

We approach the house, Sal first, then me. He passes me the radio and sneaks ahead to the sundeck, gripping his club with both hands and holding it in front of him. Then he creeps to one side of the patio doors and slaps his back against the wall. With a sudden kick he slams open the sliding screen, points his weapon and leaps inside.

From where I stand on the deck ramp I hear nothing, see nothing. Sal is gone a long time. I picture him writhing on the floor in his own blood, his skull split by fatal blows from his own club: the end of Sal. *Oh yes ...* but not like that.

Finally he steps out onto the deck, alive and whole. He throws the club over a rail, his face grim. 'There's two of them. The girl says she knows you.' He takes the radio from my hand and leans against the rail, frowning.

I step toward him, step back, take a breath and go inside. A plum-cheeked girl is sitting on a knapsack. Not a girl really but a teenager in khaki pants, sweatshirt and hiking boots, her tousled hair cut short.

Margot.

She stands and stretches, nipples jutting under her shirt. 'Hi there,' she yawns at me.

Slowly I walk up to her and put my hands on her shoulders. The top of her head comes up to my eyes – how much she's grown! I move to kiss her cheek but she jerks away. 'This is Neil.' She stops in front of a slouching boy who seems a few years older. Still wearing his knapsack, he looks like a sway-backed horse in harness. 'My friend,' she explains. Then she turns and faces me. 'I heard Dad saying you were probably here, so we decided to visit you. That guy in the store told us how to find the house, I didn't remember where it was.'

'What if your father was wrong, what if I wasn't here? How could you travel all that way without getting in touch with me first?'

'There wasn't time.' She walks around the table with a loud step. 'Anyway, we always could've stayed on the beach and hung around, it looks like a nice place for a holiday.'

'What about school?'

'Oh, that.' She rolls her eyes. 'It's almost summer break time anyway.'

I fall into the rocking chair and its rear leg slips out of place. My right side sinks down and falls back. 'The chair,' I say foolishly. 'It's broken.'

Neil's knapsack hits the floor. He pulls out a recorder, sits down cross-legged and starts to play. 'Isn't he good?' Margot says. She kicks off her boots and does a slow circling dance through all the rooms. 'I can't believe I'm really here.' She dances up to Neil and puts her hands on his knees. 'My parents fell in love in Onlyville. Isn't that romantic?'

From behind, the door opens, the floor creaks. Sal says, 'Who are these kids?'

I turn in the rocker and bob my arm at the youngsters. 'That's my brother's daughter, Margot. That's her friend Neil on the recorder.'

Sal only glances at them. 'How long are they staying?'

'We haven't gotten to that yet.'

Margot parks herself beside me and lifts her chin. 'Who's the big lug?' she asks.

I wince. 'My ex-boyfriend.'

'Ex, my ass,' Sal says.

'How long is *he* staying?'

A pain ticks between my eyes. Sal sits down at the kitchen table and fingers the keys of his typewriter. Margot flops on the sofa with her legs dangling over the arm. Neil is playing Telemann. I squirm in the rocking chair and try to sit up straighter. 'We have to settle a few things first,' I begin. 'Margot, does your father know you're out here?'

She and Neil exchange looks. Neil blows a deep note and puts the recorder in his lap.

'Don't tell.'

'I have to,' I say. 'He's probably called the cops by now.'

Margot hides her face in her hands. 'You said you'd be there any time I needed you, you said you cared. Now you want to send me back and you don't even know what's going on!'

I push out of the rocker and move toward her, seeing her as an eight-year-old with plum cheeks and tangled hair who liked to bite off split ends and spit them into her open palms. Remembering the feel of her hair when I looped it around my fingers; the smell of her scalp. I kneel by the couch and pull her hands away from her face. 'I have to tell him where you are but I'll ask him to let you stay awhile. How's that?'

'He won't listen.'

'I think he will.'

Neil says, 'Today's Margot's birthday.'

'La-de-da,' Sal says.

I stand up and go outside. Sal follows me over to Atlantic and The Boulevard and half inside the phone booth. I elbow him back and shut the door.

I call collect. A woman on the other end accepts the charges. 'Just a minute,' she says smoothly, then I hear Jay on the line. 'Hello?'

'It's Anna. How are you?'

'Margot's gone. Have you heard from her?'

'She's here with me in Onlyville. She's okay.'

Silence, then, 'I told Sal I thought that's where he'd find you.'

'Why did she do it? What's wrong?'

Another pause. 'Did she come alone?'

'With a friend.'

'Neil?'

'He seems nice.'

'A drop-out, a bum. She was cutting classes because of him. Now he talks her into this.'

'She wants to stay.'

'For how long?'

'I don't know. I haven't really talked to her yet.'

Muffled talk – his hand over the mouthpiece? Then, 'You mind?'

'I'll let you know.'

Finally he says, 'Today's her birthday.'

'I'm going to buy a cake when I hang up.'

Whispers in the background and Jay again: 'You think she'll be all right there?'

'I think so.'

'You'll phone again?'

'Of course I will.'

Sal is at my heels from the phone booth to the store to the frozen foods aisle where I choose a chocolate cream pie, one of Margot's favorites. 'What'd he say?' he asks. 'Is he coming for her?'

I swing away from the frosty bin, the pie box between us. 'He said she can stay.'

'You mean you're going to let her?'

'It's Jay's house too, you know. Margot has the right to stay.'

Sal groans. 'I wanted us to be alone.'

❁

‹ 29 ›

As parties go, it's not much. The pie is still half frozen long after dinner and the candles won't stand up straight. Margot shrugs at the present I give her, a silk scarf of Mother's that I found upstairs. 'It smells bad.'

'It belonged to your grandmother.'

'I didn't even know her.' She balls the scarf and stuffs it into a pocket.

Neil's gift for Margot is a long strand of black beads. She knots them around her neck and runs to look in a mirror. 'You always know what I want,' she says. 'Far out!'

Sal is checking his watch. 'Guess what time it is.'

'Late,' I yawn and start for the stairs.

But Margot skips to the sliding doors and waves us on. 'Not yet!' she calls out. 'We have to look at stars first.'

No moon. The sky is clear, a field of lights. When I crook my neck and look up there are too many stars, all equally small and intense. I can't spot a single constellation. Neil touches my arm and points. 'That's Polaris.' Then he draws a figure over his head with a finger. 'There's Draco the Dragon.'

'He knows lots of things,' says Margot, hopping onto the front rail and reaching into a pocket. A light flares and a line of smoke crosses the deck.

'You're smoking dope!'

'I know what it is,' Margot says. 'Want some?' She holds the joint out to me. When I shake my head she laughs hoarsely, smoke shooting from her mouth. 'It's only grass.'

'I'll take it.' Sal walks up to her, hand poised. He fingers the joint and drags deeply, turns and offers it to Neil.

Margot pulls his arm down. 'Neil gets high on meditation. He doesn't smoke.'

Sal has another toke and passes the joint to Margot. 'Yech,' she says, 'you slobbered all over it.'

Sal shrugs and Margot smokes – so cocky I could slap her. I think of how I punished her when she would misbehave as a child – sit-in-the-corner, go-to-your-room. How I would forgive her and call her back in minutes flat, missing her company that much.

Sal and Margot pass the joint between them now. They huddle by the rail, snickering, blocking my view of the ocean, all of a sudden the best of friends. Their stupid grins. I wish they'd never come here, either one of them.

Sal walks up to me, 'Here, Anna, try some,' and waves the joint in front of my face. His breath smells of ashes and the arm he hangs around my shoulders is heavy and warm. When I try to pull away he whispers, 'Take it easy. A couple of puffs and everything's cool.'

'I want to set a good example – Margot's only fourteen.'

'Forget that.' He puts the joint close to my lips. 'Quick, before I burn myself.'

I breathe in, holding the smoke, then cough it out. 'Again,' he says, and I puff again. In, out, in and out ... stars threading overhead like a cherub's playing join-the-dots.

Sal has a last drag and flicks the roach into the sand. Then he kisses me, exhaling smoke in my mouth. His lips are spongy-wonderful. Margot wiggles off the rail and patters up to us, giggling. She puts an arm around my waist and one around Sal's hips, and we stand as fixed and beaming as the Summer Triangle in the sky.

TWO: 1959

JAY AND BONNIE'S wedding in December was a small affair. All of us fit into two cars – the bride and groom, Bonnie's parents and younger sister, myself and Dad. We rode to City Hall for the service, over in seven minutes flat, then on to Bonnie's parents' house for wine and cheese. I remember the newlyweds two-stepping in tight circles while Jimmie Rodgers sang from the stereo 'Kisses Sweeter than Wine.' Bonnie was wearing a pleated dress to hide her swollen belly, and Jay wore a plaid suit much too big in the shoulders. He was eighteen and looked like a boy. Bonnie was only sixteen but heavy-breasted and rounded, more like an aunt or older sister than Jay's wife.

It was a somber occasion, coming so soon after Mother's death. Dad and Jay kept to opposite sides of the room. When it was time to toast the newlyweds Dad could think of nothing to say. He blinked at each of us in turn as if he'd never seen us before, as if he'd stumbled drunkenly into the wrong house. Bonnie's father leaped in, 'To the bride and groom, to their happiness,' and Bonnie's mother broke into sobs. For what sort of happiness lay ahead for a teenage mother-to-be and a grocery clerk?

I took pictures of the bride, although what I saw in the viewfinder wasn't Bonnie as she was but as I'd seen her over the years. Click! and she was fourteen, eyebrows shaved and black arches penciled in, which made her look astounded. Fifteen! her hair in a ponytail, resting her chin in her hand to show the high school ring she wore on her finger – Rupert's. Only a year later she was Jay's girl, hair cropped, face scrubbed, trying to make a good impression on Mother, but it didn't work. Bonnie crying at the cottage, Bonnie sleeping like an infant, two fingers stuck in her mouth . . . all this I remembered well. I wanted to feel something for her, my sister-in-law, Jay's wife, but she was only someone ridiculous seen through the eye of the camera.

When I aimed the lens at Jay he twitched like a frog under a microscope and I saw his skin pulled back, his red innards and sad heart. I saw his lungs fill with hope and empty again, fill and empty. He raised his arms to protect himself, and finally I turned the camera on someone else.

Dad was natty in a three-piece suit, his wavy hair trimmed at the neck but just long enough on top to be considered rakish. His right arm slightly crooked as if from the habit of always having a woman on his elbow. But he'd come to the wedding with me, not with his girlfriend. Back at the apartment there had been a scene. First someone banged on the door and when he opened it there was Helene, dressed to kill in a blue sheath. 'I'm coming,' she said.

'You're not,' he answered.

I went to my room, but their voices carried. 'This isn't the time,' Dad said. 'My wife –'

'Your wife?'

'– Jay's mother, passed away just three months.'

'He's getting married, isn't he?'

'You know how he feels about you and me . . .'

I stopped listening. This was just the start of another one of their arguments that wound up with Helene crying and Dad saying how much he wanted to marry her but couldn't when his wife was alive, and now they had to wait a decent amount of time. She always believed him in the end, and it made me feel sorry for her. But truly I was on Dad's side. I didn't think he should marry again and knew he shouldn't marry Helene-the-homewrecker, Mother's rival. *Young enough to be his daughter.*

I took a few shots of Dad and swung the camera around to Bonnie's parents. Mrs. Bruckner's makeup was smudged. She stared at Jay with a hard look. Mr. Bruckner slumped in a corner, gazing woozily into his wine. I would have liked to snap whatever he saw in his glass. Then there was that younger sister, a taller shapeless version of Bonnie, looking like a sausage in her tight dress. When I pointed the camera in her direction she ran from the room.

Only Bonnie wanted to pose for a group shot, the others had to be coaxed into line. 'Your daughter's wedding party,' I said. 'Your son's marriage.' No one touched. They stood in a row, equidistantly apart, like the tines of a fork. Dad and Jay were side by side, their eyes identically shaded with the same tinge of embarrassment.

❀

Five months later Margot was born and Bonnie started phoning me: Margot did this today, Margot did that – rolled over, sat up, crawled across the room, got her first tooth. But really she wanted to hear about my time at school, not what I was studying but about the friends and football games and high school dances she was missing out on. I was missing out on them too but didn't let on. I made up a whole life for her – girlfriends I didn't have, pajama parties I never went to, dates with boys who kissed my breasts in Chevy coupes. 'Oh,' she'd say, 'how wonderful. I can feel it.' And through her voice I felt it too, the pressure of their soft lips – but better than that, her envy.

Sometimes she'd ask me to babysit and Dad would drive me over Saturday evening. He'd drop me at the curb and go. Jay and Bonnie rented a small bungalow in a subdivision called Regency Hills where Jay worked in a supermarket chain store. When he answered my knock he always looked around first, squinting at some distant trail of dust before he'd let me in. Bonnie, in the bathroom doing her makeup, would call out 'Hi!'

One time I sat on the edge of the living room couch, my bed for the night, while Jay paced and a cockroach ran up the wall. In another room baby Margot jumped up and down in her crib, yowling.

'Where you going?' I asked Jay.

'A party. Some guys from work.' He bent down and buffed his shoes with a handkerchief. 'I want to make a good impression.'

Bonnie came out of the bathroom in a strapless dress that seemed a size too small. Her eyes were black with liner and mascara and her lids sparkled silvery-blue. Jay said, 'For chrissake, why do you have to look like that?'

She ignored him. She swept in and out of the baby's room, closing the door behind her. The howling went on, slightly muffled. Bonnie waggled up to the couch, her heels clicking against the floor, and grinned at me, a smear of red lipstick on her front tooth. 'Sometimes I just feel like I could grab hold of that kid and *I don't know what.*' She turned to Jay, 'Let's go,' and swung a shawl across her shoulders, saying on her way out, 'Lucky it's a warm night. I don't even have a good coat.'

I stayed in the living room watching TV, the volume turned up high. Behind the set a pair of roaches scurried up the wall abreast, right, left and loop-the-loop. But Margot's crying got to me. I went to her room, lifted her out of the crib and rocked her in my arms. She had four teeth, fat cheeks and sprigs of hair; her eyes were scrunched and watery. Not so pretty, but nice to hold. I carried her back to the living room, settled her on my lap and together we watched the late show.

In the morning Bonnie stayed in bed and Jay drove me back home. He was driving too fast, weaving in and out of lanes as I clung to the armrest. When traffic suddenly slowed and the car in front of us stopped short, Jay hit the brakes and I thumped against the dashboard. 'You'll kill us!' I screamed.

His hands slid off the steering wheel and his shoulders collapsed, his face as gray as the pavement. 'She made an ass of herself last night,' he said.

'Bonnie did?'

'Shoving her tits in people's faces, grinding her hips!'

The traffic started moving again. I rolled down a window and breathed the stale heavy air that signaled we had crossed the city limits. 'Mother never liked her,' he said. 'She said I was too innocent for my own good.'

'I won't live in a cell,' Bonnie spoke into the telephone one afternoon. 'The bungalow is bad enough.' Months earlier Jay had shown her plans for a bomb shelter, an eight-by-ten-foot basement room with a chemical toilet and folding cots. 'I laughed at him,' she told me, 'and he yelled at me, "Don't you know there's strontium 90 in Margot's milk!" Is there, Anna?'

'Probably.'

'Then he started bringing home these concrete blocks and lumber, he was banging around the basement for weeks. After that it was kerosene and batteries, but I won't put a foot in there, it looks too much like prison. It's his room now anyway, he shuts himself in and we don't see him for hours on end. Sometimes he even sleeps there.' Her voice sharpened, 'Makes no difference to me where he sleeps but I get so mad thinking how we could've used that money for really good things.' Her tone changed to dreamy. 'I always wanted to see California,' she said.

The next time I babysat I crept down to the basement to investigate the shelter. I entered through a steel door and tripped on a garbage can before I found a lamp in the main room. It threw a hard light on the walls, on three cots and a table. There were shelves with single rows of books, canned goods and water jugs. Clock and radio, flashlight and tools – everything hooked or strapped into place. I sat down on the edge of a cot. At the foot of the bed was a small shelf with two framed photographs, one of Margot, one of Mother, faraway looks on their faces, as if they were trapped in another dimension. Staring at them I knew what it was like to be Jay, sitting alone in your fallout room as if the Bomb had already dropped and the world you knew had ended, crying over snapshots of your mother and child.

Two years later I would think of the shelter again when I checked into my room on a New England campus: harsh light, cell-sized. When I unpacked photographs I'd snatched from the family album – one of Mother on Dad's lap and a blurred shot of Mother, Jay and me standing shoulder to shoulder, wearing ONLYVILLE T-shirts.

My roommate's name was Ida. She was tall and stooped, with hair to her shoulders half covering her pointy face. She was homesick too, though she'd brought nothing with her to remind her of her family. I knew this only because of words she doodled on her desk pad – *Mummy, Daddy, Baby Louie, Maryann.* She never would have told me such a personal thing. I was happy enough to talk about art and literature, to gossip about profs and fellow students. We agreed that nobody measured up, although our standards varied. Sometimes we valued differentness and sneered at boys in football uniforms, girls in pink sweater sets and the gray-suited faculty. Sometimes we valued intelligence and were sure no one was half as smart as we were. Then there were times we wished we were blond and apple-cheeked, that someone would ask us to join a sorority or the cheerleading team.

In the winter of our sophomore year Ida shared a secret with me. One night – we were studying by candlelight – she said, 'Look at this,' turning her face and pulling her hair back on one side. I swung around at my desk to stare at Ida's head. She was sitting cross-legged on her bed. She was missing an ear. A chill ran down my arms and legs. Missing an ear – like Van Gogh! Had she cut it off in a fit of passion, lost it in love? Mangled it in some brutal machine? Was she beaten, mauled or – less thrilling – born that way? There were no signs of mutilation, only a hole and the plane of her jaw where an ear should be.

'How did it happen?'

Ida smiled. 'What's it matter?'

I got shrill. 'Why show me at all if you're not gonna say how it happened!'

'I thought you'd want to know how really different I am.'

I waited an extra beat before I said, 'It doesn't matter.' Ida let her hair swing forward again and glanced at me from under her lids. Of course it mattered, we both knew. There was one slot for Unpopular Co-eds and another slot for Unpopular and Deformed.

'I'm still your friend,' I insisted. 'What do I care?' But something new was in my voice, something I couldn't keep out – a wobble of excitement. I tossed my head to shake it away, grateful at that moment for my two ears.

'What if I cut my hair off and everyone knew,' Ida said. 'Would you still be my friend then? Would you walk down the street with me and let people see us together?'

'Sure,' I said, imagining rows of pointing fingers: there they go, that pair of freaks. 'Sure, why not.'

She smiled again as she opened a drawer and pulled out scissors. Slowly she cut a flap of hair away from her missing ear, exposing the hole, and I yelled, 'Stop it!'

She rushed to a mirror and clipped her hair all around in a

lopsided bowl cut. I stood behind her, fists clenched. 'You don't know what you're doing,' I said. 'You're crazy.'

She wheeled around. 'All done. What do you think?' Then she laughed until the veins in her neck showed and tears squeezed out of her eyes. 'Don't tell me,' she wheezed. 'It's all over your face.' She ran out. I followed her into the corridor and watched as she fled, her shoes smacking the tiled floor. At the end of the hall she paused to look back at me, only her good ear visible, and cried out, 'I have no friends!'

I didn't move. She was making a scene. Any second now someone would stick out her head to see what all the noise was about. Would see Ida. See me. Ida's ear. One by one the doors would open, everyone would start to talk . . . No, I couldn't stand that. I went back in the room and quietly shut the door.

The floor was littered with Ida's hair. I picked up a strand and held it in my palm. Like a dead worm. A finger, a stem. Fragile and awful at the same time. Then suddenly I hated her and dropped the hair.

The next day I walked in to find her stretched out on her bed, dragging on a cigarette. A paper cup on the floor was half filled with butts. The room was thick with smoke and my throat hurt when I breathed in. I dropped my books on a chair and opened the window.

There was a gasp. A quick smell of burnt hair. When I turned around, Ida was holding a butt between her fingers and examining a red welt on her inner arm.

'What're you doing!' I jumped at her and we fought over the cigarette, which finally rolled onto the floor. 'Swear you'll never do that again.'

She closed her eyes. 'It really hurts.'

I crushed the cigarette out on the floor, then went to the bathroom to soak a cloth in cold water. When I came back I threw her the cloth – 'Here, put this over it' – and fell on my bed.

'I won't do it ever again if you stay my friend,' she whispered.

'You're crazy,' I said. 'I can't be friends with a crazy person – do what you want! It's not my business what you do.'

Soon after I changed rooms. In May I heard she'd dropped out of school, but I didn't ask why. I'm sure it had nothing to do with me. It wasn't my fault. No.

❀

I met Henry in April, 1965, and after that I had no time for roommates or anyone else. The day I first saw him he was leaning against a building in a corner of the quadrangle, watching a ring of protesters who shouted hoarsely, 'One, two, three, four, we don't want your bloody war!' A stranger on the sidelines in an Army jacket and khakis, dragging on a cigarette. I liked his silence, his separateness, the foggy smoke around his head.

I waited till he noticed me. 'Why aren't you marching?' he said.

'Too much noise.'

He said, 'You should hear it in Nam.'

'Were you – did you fight in Nam?' He nodded. I was deeply impressed: soldier, warrior, hero. 'Do you hate the war?'

'I miss my buddies back there. I miss waking up knowing every day could be my last.'

He butted out his cigarette, and something about the violent twist of his boot made me ask, 'Are you enrolled here?'

'I like to watch the action, that's all.'

I moved a step away from him. He reached out and took my elbow, 'Where can we get a drink?' and I walked beside him thinking, This is a stupid thing to do, a crazy dangerous thing. What if he's an FBI agent, a narc? A psychopath? *What if?*

But what if he's not? What if he's brave and tender-hearted, what if he's patient, sensitive, kind? What if he falls in love with me?

❀

Henry had shrapnel in his leg. During the months of our affair I studied his scars one by one, learning the shape and texture of each, the hairless skin shiny and smooth, like implanted glass through which you might see, if you looked hard, the still pulsing wound below.

Henry showed me photos he'd taken in Nam: palm trees

and paddy fields, water buffalo, thatched huts, base camp and oil drums, his buddies standing in a row, their arms around each other's shoulders; portrait of a sergeant in a mottled helmet, 'Good luck, Hank!' inscribed across the shot. Everything calm and friendly in his pictures. They made me want to be there among those soldiers dressed in green, loose-limbed and sleepy-eyed, the butt of a burning cigarette between my lips. Henry pointed out the ones who made it back, the ones who died. He did this slowly, careful not to touch and smudge the photographs.

He was only twenty-two but there was something old about Henry. How easily I could picture him fat, sinking into a sofa with his feet on a hassock, holes in his socks, his wheezy cough as he had a smoke. While three kids chased each other around a color TV and his wife busied herself in the kitchen cooking a roast.

In June we moved into one and a half rooms a short drive from campus. An unmade bed, a bare floor, a kitchenette with a half-size fridge and hot plate. Still I felt uncrowded there, unwatched, though when we were home we were never more than a few feet apart, though we ate on chairs pushed together and shared the same beanbag chair to watch TV. I was gone all day typing in the office of a furniture store. What I liked best about that summer was coming home to Henry every evening: the smell of something cooking and the drip-drip of wet laundry hanging in the shower stall. At night we lay on a narrow bed, his back turned to me and my arms around his waist while he snored, a rumbling that reminded me of the ocean.

He made love with a quick passion that seemed to have little to do with me, his thrust hard and rat-a-tat. It would end with a gasp, an explosion of breath, his body crashing onto mine. But wasn't I supposed to be sweaty and breathless too? 'Was it good?' he'd ask, and I would nod. It wasn't bad exactly, so I figured it was good enough.

After, he would always want to talk about Nam, the endless patrols: the heat, rain, mud, dust, snakes, mosquitoes, leeches and the buddy killed in a booby trap, the one cut down by sniper fire, the one who lost his nuts to a mine, the one who bled to death in his arms, the cellar-smell of jungle air, the swampy stink of rotting flesh, fear drying up your mouth, nights without sleep, nights lit up by tracers and exploding shells, the noise of artillery all night, then days and nights of nothing to do ... I was sorry for him, for what he'd been through, but the feeling he released in me was bigger than that. I felt the loss of his friends as if they were mine too.

By the end of the summer Henry wanted to move to the city – my home town – and look for a job. 'There's nothing for me here,' he said. He wanted me to quit school, live with him in a big apartment, show him around.

'This is my last year,' I said. 'Can't you wait till I graduate?'

'I can't wait.' He lit up a cigarette just then, and his face trembled slightly when he inhaled.

I pictured myself back in the dorm, my nose in a book. I pictured myself in Henry's arms, my nose in his curly chest hairs, his skin smelling of sun and smoke.

It was Mother's idea that I would go to university, not mine. Her idea that art wasn't something you did but something you studied – history. Spend your time with painters and sculptors long dead.

Or spend my time with Henry.

I followed him to the city and we got an apartment not far from where I'd gone to high school. Henry had trouble finding a job so I went to work typing again. Office temp. I'd give him time to get on his feet, then sign up at a downtown college in the spring.

At the end of 1965 Bonnie ran off with a neighbor's son, a young trucker who promised to drive her back and forth across the land. 'We're never going to stop!' she said, and her breath pulsed through the telephone wire that ran all the way from Regency Hills to where I stood ironing shirts for Henry's job interviews.

'Does Jay know?'

'I left a note.'

'And Margot?'

'I'll be back for her,' Bonnie said.

I went back to ironing, my wrist aching as I worked. Too

much ironing, too much typing, too much standing in one spot. My feet hurt, my arm was sore: I was twenty-one but felt old. *Henry,* I'd say when he got home, *something's wrong, I need a change.* And he would tumble into the sofa, put his feet up, light a cigarette, turn the TV on loud.

I'd walk into the living room. *Henry, I'm bored, I need more.* He'd pull me down and kiss me, touch me, *This is what you need, honey, this and this . . .*

So, was it good?

No, Henry, not good. There must be something better than this.

Later I got a call from Dad. I was at the ironing board again. At the sound of his voice I pushed the iron back and forth at rocket speed, the heat turned up to maximum. Was he going to chew me out again for not visiting him and Helene ('I can't believe you're *that* busy'), tell me how I owed it to him to be nice to her ('You can't even phone her once in a while?'), or blame it all on Henry ('First he makes you drop out of school, now he won't let you see anyone')?

He was calling to talk about Bonnie and Jay. 'Are you listening?'

'Uh-huh,' I said.

'Of course I didn't tell Jay, he's got enough on his mind right now, but I always thought she was scatterbrained. He never would've married her in the first place if your mother hadn't died like that.'

I stood the iron on its heel. 'She was pregnant!'

'Naturally he didn't ask what I thought – no one in this family asks me anything – but if he did I would've said, "Don't do it, she's not for you." I would've given him the name of a doctor too. Then it wouldn't have come to this, Bonnie run off and Jay crying to me on the phone.'

'A doctor? You told him that?'

'No, I didn't tell him *that,*' he mimicked me. 'What I said was, "How come I only hear from you when you're in trouble? Otherwise you don't know me, you're like your sister – too busy."'

After his call I couldn't get back to ironing. Bonnie was on my mind again, Bonnie traveling west with a hunk while I was here holding up the ass of a man who couldn't get a job or, when he got one, couldn't keep it. Who, if he didn't quit first, would soon be fired for lack of interest – and it was true, everything bored him, manual labor, sales, management, office work. On his applications he would write under *Experience*, 'jungle warfare,' under *Interests*, 'automatic rifles.' Really he was suited to a life of crime, but he wanted something respectable, with regular hours.

I set the iron down on the breast pocket of Henry's shirt and burned a hole right through. A wave of heat rose from the board, from the ruined shirt, and I thought, California! My face hot and sweaty and my pulse banging in my head. I could be sitting in the cab of a truck on the highway *right now*, windows rolled down and the wind in my hair. Going somewhere, on the move, no one holding me back anymore. On my own!

But where would I go? And what would I do when I got there – office temp? No profession, no apartment, no one to come home to. *On my own.* I grabbed hold of the ironing board. The charred smell of Henry's shirt was the stink of fear.

Bonnie must be out of her mind.

I phoned Jay in Regency Hills. 'Jay,' I said, 'I heard what happened. What she did.'

He started to speak but his voice cracked. Then there was a thud – the phone? – and Margot on the line. 'Mommy? Is that you?'

'No, sweetie, it's Aunt Anna.'

'Where's Mommy?'

'I don't know.'

Background whispers and Jay again, 'I can talk now.'

'It's okay.'

'It's *not* okay,' his voice going up. 'It's not just me, it's Margot too – a five-year-old! Who's going to take care of her all day?'

'Bonnie's mother?'

'We don't get along.'

'Then you'll have to hire someone.'

'How can a mother walk out on her own kid?' He was shouting now. 'It's not only me – not me – !'

After that I just listened and soon his voice gave out again.

When I hung up I was teary-eyed. How could Bonnie hurt him like that? How could she leave Margot? Hop in a truck and go nowhere, for no good reason, giving up her family and friends and everything familiar. I ran a finger around the rim of the hole I'd made in Henry's shirt. Anything could happen to Bonnie. Terrible things.

I bundled up his white shirt and stuffed it into the garbage. I'd buy Henry another shirt – a better shirt – tomorrow.

Henry took an aptitude test that pointed to a career as a gunsmith or lighthouse keeper, both offering 'limited opportunities.' He took the news with good grace. Later he found work as a security guard in a museum, a job I truly envied. He thought he could stay interested in that one for a long time because he liked the uniform. In fact he was still there in May, five months later, still attentive, proud of himself, settled down.

One evening, suppertime, he slammed open the kitchen window to let in warm gusts of air. Street sounds and baby-cries blew into the room as we sat knee to knee eating 'Beans Mexicana' from a recipe I'd found on a can of Hunt's tomato sauce. 'Tastes like C-rations,' Henry said, but his tone was sweet, and when I glanced at him I caught the twitch of a smile on his lips. Quickly I swallowed a mouthful of rice as he leaned forward and kissed me, his tongue tasting of chili. Something moved in the corner of my eye then, a solitary centipede or cockroach running up the wall, and I felt sad. I kissed him back more forcefully and longer than I meant to. The sound of howling babies rose, like an orchestra crescendo at the end of a show.

'I want to know something,' he said. 'Will you marry me?'

The room throbbed. I saw myself taking a picture of Henry and a line of kids, boys in helmets, black-haired girls in conical hats, everyone's arms around each other's shoulders. The children were familiar to me – their fat cheeks and startled eyes – but also unfamiliar. The camera shaking in my hands: the print would be blurred.

'I want us to start a family and move away from the city,

have a real life,' Henry said. 'Think about it, okay? Don't answer right away.'

I thought about it but couldn't decide. Yes, but not with Henry. (Find a more dependable guy, someone with direction.) No, not with anyone. (Finish school and make something of yourself.) Yes, Henry, yes! (You'll never be lonely again.)

He didn't bring it up again. He grew quiet and chain-smoked. I was extra nice to him, cooked his favorite suppers, cuddled up to him and darned his socks. Buying time.

Yes, no. Yes. No.

In June he quit the museum and said he was moving on – nothing for him here anymore. He didn't ask me to come along, he only said, 'The apartment's paid till the end of the month.'

'But I haven't made up my mind yet.'

'I made up mine.'

'It's my decision – not yours. You can't just go!'

He was already packed. Even then I might have changed his mind, I could've thrown myself in his arms and cried, 'I'll marry you!' My muscles tensed, ready to spring, but my feet were weighted down when I stood in the hall and watched him move from landing to landing down the stairs, like someone caught in a whirlpool. My lips parted and puckered up like they were already missing him and wanted to call him back, but I didn't speak.

I went inside the apartment and looked around: no trace of Henry. Nothing forgotten, nothing left behind as a memento. Not a card or photograph, not even a dirty sock. The emptiness of the place took my breath away.

From the bathroom I heard the drip of a faucet and slapped my hands over my mouth. *What have I done?*

July was a hot month. Under the flat tar roof of the bungalow in Regency Hills I thought about Bonnie perched above the traffic in the cab of a truck, bouncing on a leather seat while the Beach Boys sang on the radio. While I was stirring Cream of Wheat, three level tablespoons to a cup of boiling water, and fanning myself with morning papers folded over grim headlines, MORE TROOPS TO VIETNAM, DEATH TOLL RISING, and a picture of a dead soldier lying on his back with his helmet off and upturned like a soup bowl. Did Henry – wherever he was – see that photo too? Was it someone he knew? Someone he would cry over? Someone he'd miss?

When Jay was gone and the table cleared, I put a load in the washing machine and turned on the TV. Margot flopped down at my feet with a coloring book and crayons. On a talk show three women were discussing *The Feminine Mystique* and the desperation of young housewives stuck in their suburban homes with babies and appliances.

'I want to watch cartoons,' said Margot.

'I'm watching something now.'

'This is when I watch cartoons. Mrs. Mueller lets me.'

'Mrs. Mueller doesn't work here anymore, I'm taking care of you now. You can watch when it's your turn.'

She grabbed a crayon and rushed at the set, at the mouth of Dr. So-and-so saying words like 'self-esteem' and 'self-realization,' dabbing the screen with dots and dashes, like Morse code. I grabbed Margot by the waist and yanked her back. She fell kicking and punching, and I hooked my arms and legs around her, clamping her still. 'You're not Mommy,' she panted, 'and I don't have to listen to you!'

I let go of her at once and went to stand by an open window, to stare at sunlight hopping off the hoods and roofs of parked cars, to watch the broken line that split the black road. A smell of tar and rubber and exhaust fumes: I felt sick. From the TV a stern voice: 'The rise of black nationalism, the rise of student activism . . .'

What the hell am I doing *here*?

After lunch we went for a walk. I swear there wasn't a tree in the neighborhood more than seven feet tall and none of them threw enough shade to fill a jar. The sidewalks were new, the white frame houses new, the lawns yellow-brown in spots but mowed, edged and litter-free. Nothing restful to the eye and no sound but the sudden whoosh of a passing car. We covered most of Regency Hills, one street the same as the next, heading for a playground at the end of the development. Here there was a water fountain, monkey bars and slides and a row of swings. We drank from the fountain and sat on a bench under the branch of a young birch. 'Go play if you like,' I said, but Margot only shook her head, 'It's too hot.'

Everything in the playground seemed to radiate heat – chains and rungs, bars and handles. I closed my eyes and willed September into mind, the start of classes, turning of leaves, the cool nights. I could reapply now for the spring term.

Across the park a woman pushed a baby swing with a regular sluggish motion, as if she couldn't stop herself or speed up. Another woman passed by carrying an infant on her shoulder. She was young, maybe my age, with a helmet of dark teased hair, dressed in shorts and a sleeveless top, a bra strap showing. Margot bounded to her feet and called 'Mommy!' The young mother blinked at us and walked on.

I grabbed Margot's hand and we caught a bus to the local pool, surprisingly empty in mid-afternoon. Neither one of us knew how to swim so we sat still in the shallow end, staring at our private, separate visions in the water.

August was unpredictable in Regency Hills, hot and muggy one day, chilly, wet and windy the next. And like the weather, we were changeable, quiet and tired or stormy. Margot had a string of tantrums – wouldn't go to bed on time or drink her milk or put away toys – but then would circle the house silently, moving from window to window. After weeks of not mentioning Bonnie's name she started asking for her again: 'Where's Mommy? Why is she taking so long?' Jay would come home from work and crash through the bungalow kicking toys, muttering about his boss, some half-wit customer, his hateful wife – or else he'd slip through the front door and creep to his room unnoticed.

On a warm, drizzly afternoon I hoisted Margot onto my lap and opened *The Velveteen Rabbit*. I began reading, liking the feel of her on my knee and how she burrowed into my shoulder, crying for the toy rabbit tossed aside. Her hair shone; it smelled of soil and cut grass. 'It has a happy ending,' I said. 'A fairy makes the rabbit real.'

She hugged my arm. 'Real like us, me and you?'

'Yes,' I said. I had become real too. Just then.

Someone knocked at the front door. I closed the book and took Margot's hands in mine – 'We don't have to answer' – but she yanked away and ran to the door.

'Mommy,' she cried, 'you came back!'

Bonnie stood in the doorway wearing bell-bottom jeans and a fringed vest. Her hair was stringy, her makeup nearly rubbed off. Margot threw herself against her mother's legs, and Bonnie peered down at her with sleepy eyes. 'Shut the door,' I said sharply, but no one paid attention to me.

They fell on the couch in a huddle, murmuring, 'Mommy's little bunny-wunny, Mommy's own,' 'Don't ever go again, promise.' I went to close the front door and saw a large van at the curb. A young long-haired man was smoking in the cab. When I turned around, Bonnie was braiding Margot's hair.

'She doesn't like it like that,' I said.

'Yes I do!' said Margot.

Bonnie squinted and scanned me slowly, head to foot. I wished I hadn't done my hair in a ponytail that morning. I wished I wasn't wearing a plaid short set. She said, 'What're you doing here?'

'Looking after your daughter.'

'Anna to the rescue!' Bonnie leaned back, pulling Margot's head onto her lap. 'Is Auntie Anna-fanna taking good care of Mommy's own?' Bonnie rubbed the girl's head and curled her hair around her fingers. 'Mommy loves her bunny more than anyone in the whole world.'

'You're drunk,' I said.

'Drunk? No one gets drunk anymore. I'm a little stoned, no big deal.' She waved me off. 'Why don't you go make coffee or something?'

In the kitchen I had to sit down, I felt faint. The coffeepot on the counter was a tower of dots. They were cooing in the next room, a soft and intimate babbling. I didn't want to listen, but I couldn't stop.

Outside a horn blared. Margot yelled 'No!' and I ran to her. Bonnie was on her feet again, Margot crouched beside her with her arms around her mother's leg. 'That's my old man calling,' Bonnie said. 'Gotta move.'

'You can't go!' Margot cried.

Bonnie dropped to one knee and cupped the girl's face in her hands. 'The way we live's not for a kid. You have to go to school soon, you can't move around like us.'

'Don't go!'

'Bunny, I'll be back for you, don't cry. We're saving up and soon we'll live in a big house, you, me and Julius. A real house three stories high.'

'I don't want another house, I want you to stay!'

The horn again, louder this time. 'Bonnie,' I said, 'you can't come and go like this – *you just can't.*' She shook herself free of Margot, shoved me aside and ran out. I watched her scuttle into the truck and speed away.

Margot wouldn't let me near. She went to her room and slammed the door. When Jay came in the house was still, Margot holed up in her room and me on the couch. 'What's that smell?' Jay asked, sniffing smoke and ashes. He looked in the kitchen and living room, behind the drapes and under a chair. 'Who was here?' He opened the front door, took a step outside, came in again. 'Where's Margot?'

'In her room.'

He turned toward the bedroom and I stood up. 'Don't go in there right now, she wants to be alone,' but his hand was on the doorknob. When he twisted it I burst out, 'Bonnie was here – out of the blue.'

He paused. 'You mean you let her in? You let her speak to Margot?'

'For godssake, she's her mother!'

Then he was in the bedroom with the door shut. I heard Margot whimpering, the angry pitch of Jay's voice, the tinkling crash of something thrown and broken. Moments later Jay exploded from the room, his freckles black as pinholes. He yanked open the front door and left it ajar. I saw him on the street with his fists beating the evening sky. 'I'll kill her!' he screamed. 'The fuckin' bitch!' Along the block the front door of every bungalow opened a crack and the eyes of our neighbors peeked out.

Then it was fall. All across Regency Hills cedars and yews were carefully pruned, and maple leaves that fell in the night were put in bags set on the curb by morning.

On Halloween the streets were dotted with grownups checking their children's candy – someone was supposedly putting razor blades in apples – and the night seemed airless and grim. But Jay was in a good mood. He put on a mask and Harlequin suit just like Margot's, and they clutched hands as they left the house. I watched them skipping down the block, as identical in their movements as they were in their costumes, Margot's voice gruff with joy as she sang out 'Trick or treat!' I thought, That's the way it is when daughters hold their fathers' hands, when sisters play with big brothers. How easy to win a girl's devotion.

They ran from door to door, and I felt I was watching from a long way off.

A few nights later he came in at one a.m. and lurched to the fridge. I turned off the TV and walked up to him, arms crossed. 'Where've you been?'

'You're not my fuckin' wife,' said Jay.

'Drinking again?'

'I had a date, ooh-la-la!' He wiggled his hips. 'Want to hear? I'll tell you about it, blow by blow.'

'No,' I said.

'Want to hear what it's like to be in someone's arms and so excited you can't breathe?'

I turned to go but he blocked my way.

'Was that how it was with Henry – so excited you couldn't breathe?' The corner of his mouth went up in a crooked smile. What did he know? 'Do you miss the way he touched you? Do you miss the feel of his body?'

'Out of my way,' I said, shoving past him, but he caught my wrist.

'Maybe you're just frigid,' he said. 'Maybe you never felt a thing.'

My pulse went crazy in his grip. I don't know what he saw in my face, but suddenly he dropped my wrist and backed off.

In the morning he was sorry. 'I shouldn't have said the

things I said.' He waited but I didn't respond. 'So I guess you'll be going back to college in the spring.'

'Guess so.'

&

I took Margot to visit Dad in his office. He worked in a building closer to Regency Hills than his apartment was, but still a bus and train ride away. We got there thirty minutes late. At the end of a hall on the fifth floor Margot reached up to touch the gold letters on his door, E. BERMAN, CERTIFIED ELECTROLOGIST. Inside we sat on chrome and vinyl chairs in the waiting room. The door to the second room was closed.

I'd been here many times before and was no longer interested in the view of the street or the pictures hanging on the walls. But this was Margot's first trip to Grandfather's office and she stood a long time by the windows, naming vehicles that she saw, an ambulance, a garbage truck and police car. Then she moved from picture to picture, studying them as if they weren't dime-store reproductions but fine art: here a smiling woman with an infant on her shoulder while another youngster hugs her leg, there a girl playing dress-up in a trailing coat and high heels. I had the urge to draw goatees on all those beaming faces.

'That one looks like me,' said Margot, pointing to the round-eyed girl in oversized clothes. 'This one's you.' She meant the woman half covered with children, but she was wrong. That one more resembled Mother, green-eyed and distracted. I might have been the babe-in-arms and Jay the little boy clinging to her leg – portraits of a family album. Dad's album. The disappearing members of his family.

The door to the inner room opened and a woman entered the waiting room. Her chin was pink and she moved in a flurry, thrusting her arms into her coat and whirring past us into the hall. Dad stood in the doorway, looking clinical in his white smock. 'You're late,' he said, frowning. 'I can give you twenty minutes. There's another patient coming at five.'

Margot took my hand as we followed him into his office, a room that smelled of lotion and alcohol, harsh and sweet, unchanged since the days of my childhood. Days when I would fidget in the waiting room, sliding from one chair to the next to see if they all felt the same, moving from window to window to compare views. 'Sit still!' Mother would bark, or if she was in a better mood she might just ignore me and talk to Jay. Suddenly Daddy would appear and I'd perk up. He'd lead us into that dusky room with the gray machine, foot pedal and black cords, the smells that made my nose itch. Later he'd take us out to lunch. If Mother and Daddy were getting along everyone talked at once about the food and weather, friends and relations, but if it was one of their bad days nobody said a word. Under the table I'd touch his hand.

'Look around,' Dad said from behind his desk. He meant Margot, not me. She glanced at the blinds, half closed, at the epilator and two stools, at a white reclining chair on a pedestal, a lamp aimed at its headrest. 'What do you think?' he asked her.

She was at my side, still holding my hand as we leaned against the huge desk. 'Looks like the dentist's.'

He motioned to the white chair, 'Come lie down.' She shook her head. 'Just for fun, see what it's like. I'll shine that big light at you and let you look through a magnifying glass – would you like that?'

I would have liked that in her place, but Margot slipped behind me. Dad got out of his seat and brought the stools over. 'Sit down a minute.' He slid into his chair again and looked at Margot sternly.

'How's Helene?' I said to change the subject.

He hunched forward. 'Not the easiest person to live with, since you asked, but that's how it goes.' He spread his arms on top of the desk. 'She thinks you don't like her, that's why you never come around.'

'Well,' I said, letting the word fill the space between us.

'I want you to visit me in my home. I want you to see us together like we're not a pair of monsters.'

'I'm too busy right now.'

'Busy, busy – that's all I ever get from you.' His voice softened: 'I remember when you always had time for me.'

I looked away. And you for me, I was thinking.

He fell back in his swivel chair. 'First it's Henry, now her –

now *she* takes up all your time.' He shook his head at Margot. 'She's not your responsibility. It's not your fault her mother ran off with a longhair. Instead of going back to school you go live in the same bungalow Bonnie ran away from. Where's your sense?'

Margot slumped down in her seat and drew up her knees. I touched her arm. 'She's Jay's child too, you know – your granddaughter.'

'He talks to me when he's in trouble, that's it. You think I owe him anything? You think he's right?' He thumped a fist against his chest. 'It's not right.'

'I thought you could take her to lunch sometime, get to know her.'

He winced. 'I couldn't.'

'Busy – right?' I pulled Margot to her feet. 'Come on,' I said, 'I'm sure our twenty minutes are up.'

In the corridor she hugged my waist. 'Stay with me?' she whispered.

'I will,' I said.

❀

In April Bonnie's mother turned up unannounced. She stood in the doorway, hugging a doll, then gave it to me. 'For Margot.'

'Come in,' I said. 'Margot will be home any minute.'

Mrs. Bruckner walked in, poised on stiletto heels. She was built like a lollipop, a round body on skinny legs, but kept her balance anyway. Her feet were probably killing her. 'I was just passing by,' she said. 'I can't stay.'

I straddled the arm of the sofa and looked up at her powdered face. 'Have you heard from Bonnie?'

'No,' then, 'just once. She stopped by the house on her way somewhere, not for long.'

I closed the doll's eyes and smoothed her pigtails. 'Is she coming back?'

Mrs. Bruckner stamped one of her narrow heels against the floor. 'This whole thing was a lousy mistake, they never should've married in the first place!'

'Margot misses her mother,' I said.

'She's got you, doesn't she? And I could visit her more if she wants. How many mothers does she need?' Mrs. Bruckner threw up her hands and marched around in a circle, her heels drilling into the floor. 'I know it's wrong, a terrible thing, but what can I do? I talk to her, I tell her it's wrong, she does what she wants. You think I like the way she lives? Not that this was paradise, but at least I knew where to send her mail!' She drew a breath and her voice dropped. 'I slapped her, I did, and she ran out. Who knows if I'll ever see her again?' Her eyes teared. Mascara ran over the lower lids, shading the hollows underneath as dark as a pair of shiners.

I heard the school bus pull up. 'Baby!' Mrs. Bruckner said as Margot ran in. 'Come give your Granny a hug.'

Margot looked from me to the doll and didn't move.

'See the pretty doll?' Mrs. Bruckner pointed. 'That's for you.'

'Does she wet herself?' Margot asked.

'Well, no.'

'Talk?'

'No.'

'Walk?'

'No.'

'I don't want her.'

Mrs. Bruckner turned to me. 'You're spoiling her.' Then to Margot, 'Give me a hug anyway.'

'I don't want to,' Margot said.

To me again: 'Who turned her against her own grand-mother, you or Jay?'

'We had nothing to do with it.'

Mrs. Bruckner clattered up to Margot on her high heels and said, 'Don't you like your Granny?'

Margot stared at the floor.

'Do you want me to buy you Betsy Wetsy?'

'I don't care.'

'What *do* you want?'

Margot looked up at her and Mrs. Bruckner turned red.

Bonnie sent letters from the Coast addressed to Margot, one

that spring, one in summer, another in September. No return addresses, just the postal stamps. I kept the letters to myself. For the girl's sake, I reasoned – why get her upset? Anyway, they were foolish. The first began, 'My dollie, you were born with the sun in Gemini, the moon in Virgo . . .' What would a child make of that? The next was signed, 'Tune in, turn on, drop out!' and included a shot of Bonnie in a tie-dyed shirt reading MAKE LOVE, NOT WAR, hearts and daisies painted on her smiling face. The last letter: 'Weather good but too many people moving in, not enough food to go around . . . Stacey had a bad trip . . . Julius burned his draft card.' Then in November a postcard with an aerial view of the Golden Gate Bridge: 'Julius left but don't worry, found work. How's school? Can you read yet?'

I could've shown Margot the photograph, at least that, and I meant to. But she brought home a birthday card she'd made for me in school, and I couldn't bring myself to do it after that. I bunched the letters and stashed them away. Eventually I thought about them less and less, then not at all.

There were months of screaming headlines in the winter and spring of '68 – COMMUNIST FORCES TAKE HUÉ, MARTIN LUTHER KING KILLED, NATIONAL STUDENT STRIKE FOR PEACE – and page after page about Black Power, women's lib, gay rights. The world seemed to be happening in another place, without me, spinning out of reach while I stayed put and read about it, dreaming I was part of it. But Henry was gone and Jay too old to be drafted; I didn't know any gays or blacks or radical women either, and I wasn't a student anymore. The news had nothing to do with me. I put the papers down and picked up nineteenth-century novels. I started doing sketches too, pencil scenes of Regency Hills, those bungalows on quarter-acre lots as far as you could see. Like a row of encyclopedias on a shelf, they were quieting.

In May I shopped for things for Margot's birthday. On the big day I baked a cake in the shape of an eight, which isn't hard to do if you have a tube pan. It came to me as I iced the cake that I might've done things differently: I might have finished university, got a job in some museum, rented a small apartment close to where I worked. I might have liked my co-workers, might even have married one . . . As I licked frosting from a spoon, Margot stepped in front of me and tugged me down to her height. She said, 'The cake's beautiful,' then pressed her nose against mine. 'I love you,' she said, and watched to see what would happen – tears as big as gumdrops and a look that promised *I would do anything for you.* Satisfied, she turned on her heel and went to flounce in front of a mirror, admiring her party dress.

Seven girls from Margot's class walked in, six of them in starched dresses, one in a tie-dyed dress and beads, her hair twisting down to her waist. That was Star. 'She used to be a Susan,' Margot whispered to me.

'I don't know why she changed it,' I said. 'Susan's a perfectly good name.'

After pin-the-tail-on-the-donkey, after musical chairs, Kool-Aid, ice cream and birthday cake, Jay came in holding a box. He was grinning so hard his freckles were lost in the folds of his face. Margot was busy opening presents – books and games and Barbie clothes. Star's gift was a headband. Mine was a quilt of cotton squares I'd sewn by hand, each with an appliquéd design. Margot bunched the quilt aside and tore into Jay's gift – cowboy boots, a long skirt, a shirt in psychedelic colors. She kicked off her shoes and pulled on the boots.

'Far out!' Star said.

I looked at Jay. 'Not exactly "Regency Hills."' He put a finger to his lips and shushed me.

When everyone left and Margot and I collapsed on the floor, he knelt at his daughter's feet and rubbed her new boots with his sleeve. 'How would you like to take these boots to California?'

'Where's that?'

'As far west as you can go.'

'On the San Andreas fault,' I said.

'You'll like it there,' he told her, 'it's a good place. I'm going to start my own store and never have to work for anyone else again.'

'You won't be assistant manager anymore?'

'I'll be the boss. My own organic food store.'

'Organic?' Margot asked.

'Natural. No chemicals. Understand?'

She pouted, 'But I don't want to leave my friends.'

'California's full of little girls your age, with lots of sunny beaches you can play on.'

'Like Onlyville?'

'Better than that.'

'Is that where Mommy lives? Are we going to stay with Mommy?'

'I don't know where your mother lives. We're not going because of her.'

'How will she find us if we move?'

'We'll send our new address to Grandma, how's that? Grandma can give it to her.'

She tipped her head to consider this, then climbed into my lap. 'Did you buy Anna boots too?'

Jay stood up and moved to the window, looking out at the curled leaves of young maples dotting the street. Regency Hills wasn't half bad in spring. The air was fresh, the opening of buds sweet and intimate. 'She wouldn't want to come,' he said.

'We can't leave Anna!' Margot said.

'She's been here nearly two years, it's time for her to move on. She has to find her own life.'

'But Daddy . . .'

With every word I became smaller, sinking into the birthday litter on the floor. Losing air, becoming flat. A flat balloon. Then I was even flatter than that, paper-thin. A cut-out doll no one played with anymore.

THREE: 1970

MOVING AGAIN: stuffing sacks and cardboard boxes, loading a van. The mover has freckles and jug ears and promises not to break the lamp. Later he buys me draft beer, explains that he married too young, he didn't know any better, now he's stuck with her, the wrong girl, what can he do. He takes my hand and admires my fingers. No, it isn't sex I need, it's a fixed address.

I'd answered an ad in a weekly paper, 'Three women need fourth to share large apartment,' and was moving into a group apartment uptown. Meg and Gladys, who owned the lease, were ten years older than I was, and I was three years older than the third woman, Olivia, a grad student in English lit. They were standing in the foyer when I got there, lined up like members of a receiving line. 'Give us a hand?' the mover asked, but no one budged. 'Great bunch of friends you got,' he said to me as I lugged a box of books to my room. When I came back to the foyer my new roommates had disappeared.

❋

Meg was a potter, her room crammed with different-colored plates and planters, chunky, delicate, coarse and smooth. She invited me to look around and stood stiffly while I did, her hands in her overalls, her eyes blinking rapidly behind her round glasses. She was like a friendly farmer. After that I would often find a reason to wander into her room and sit on her old cane rocker, ringed by pots, feeling as cool and porous as clay.

Gladys was a painter. She had a large work table in her room, a grid-lined canvas on top, and next to the canvas jars of paint and short strings. Once she let me watch as she dipped a string in black paint, then dropped it onto a square of the canvas already covered with dark strings like twisted worms preserved in tar. Her jeans and shirt were spattered in black paint too, in what seemed to me a more interesting pattern than the one I saw on the canvas. 'What do you think?' Gladys asked, stepping back from the table.

'Yes,' I said, 'it has a certain primitive ...'

She frowned.

'– not *too* primitive – animation. It wiggles, like.'

Her brow uncreased. 'You mean the movement – you feel the movement.'

'Yes,' I agreed, the strings inching round and round in wormy circles under my gaze, 'the movement. I think this is an important work.'

Meg and Gladys had rooms on either side of mine. Late at night I would hear footsteps passing by my bedroom door – Meg going to Gladys' room or Gladys on her way to Meg's. I tried not to think about what they did in each other's rooms, but sometimes, half asleep, I pictured Meg in the cane rocker, Gladys curled up on her lap. I could almost hear the tender sigh of Meg's breath, the pat of her hand on Gladys' back, the thump and groan of Gladys falling off and rolling out of my dream.

On Saturday Olivia asked me to go shopping. I felt proud. Chosen by Olivia, who Gladys called a beacon of hope, a leader-in-the-making of a new generation of liberated females. Who had picketed the Miss America pageant in Atlantic City and chucked her bra in a trash can. I dressed in jeans and a sweatshirt – braless! – hoping to match Olivia's liberated look. To my surprise she came to my room in a blouse and skirt and raincoat, disappointingly ordinary after all.

She led me through department stores, the busier the better, at a wild pace, never pausing long enough for me to try on anything or even read a label. Finally I stopped dead in Hosiery. 'I need stockings,' I said in my firmest voice. (I was working office temp again till something better came up and went through a couple of pairs a week.)

'Meet you outside then.' She didn't even slow down.

I bought the stockings in a rush. On the street I saw her down the block and hurried to catch up. Next stop, the A&P. We raced through aisles and past the checkout, nothing bought. I was out of breath by then and angry – what was the point of all this?

Back in the apartment Olivia motioned me into her room and locked the door. She took off her coat and spread it open on her bed. The lining bulged. She pulled out lipstick, scissors, socks, a book of poems, then reached under her blouse for a package of steaks. 'For supper. Will you join me?'

I stared at her. 'You stole that.'

'I don't call it that, I call it "redistributing the wealth."'

I looked at the booty on the bed. 'What if you got caught? I'd be your accomplice!'

She tossed the steaks onto a chair. 'This is for you,' handing me the lipstick. 'I don't use makeup anymore.'

I shook my head. 'No thanks.'

'The markup on this stuff is really outrageous. If CEOs can rip us off, we can do the same to them.'

'I don't want it anyway.'

She reached for my hand and put the lipstick in my palm. 'A gift,' she said.

I glanced down: Watermelon. A color I looked good in.

House meetings were Thursday evenings, eight to ten, in the living room. I always brought string to knot, which gave me something to do with my hands and kept me from having to meet anyone's eyes. No one objected. Unlike knitting, macramé was politically acceptable. First on the agenda, Shopping: whose turn to buy the weekly House Staples that went into the Common Cupboard, then the collection of Grocery Money. Other Funds Now Due: Rent, Utilities, Housecleaning. Olivia, far behind in her rent, was working off her debt by being Housecleaner. Since she'd begun tidying up I'd lost a pen, a leather belt, an oversized book of Georgia O'Keeffe color plates. But I didn't accuse her, not even during Other Business or Complaints. She gave me things too, I reasoned – makeup and stockings – and anyway, I could be wrong. *Did you see her take your book?* Gladys would question me. *Have you seen her with it since then? Maybe you lent it to someone, maybe you lost it.*

Last in order was Complaints, which is when I did my fiercest knotting, making intricate plant hangers and string

bags. One evening Meg complained that Olivia wasn't clean-
ing well, the bathtub had a ring and there were dust bunnies
under her bed.

'You treat me like Cinderella,' Olivia said, 'do this, do that.
I'm a poet and a scholar and I won't waste my life on unimportant work.'

'It's not unimportant,' Meg said. 'We're paying you to do a
job we need done.'

While Meg and Olivia argued I concentrated on my knots,
the string looping around and around my fingers. I hated it
when people raised their voices. It sounded like the end of
things, like everything would shatter when the noise reached
a certain pitch.

Finally Gladys joined in, complaining that Olivia ate up
more than her share of House Staples, emptying the Common
Cupboard long before the week was through. Olivia cried that
everyone in the house was ganging up on her, including me,
who sat there saying not a word but hating her in secret. I
dropped my string.

'You see the way she never looks me in the eye,' Olivia said.

I scooped string up into my lap and buried my hands in a
hill of knots. I licked my dry lips, tasting watermelon.

'Don't you have something to say too?' Meg asked quietly.
'Something to get off your chest?'

'Me? Nope.'

'Say something!' Olivia said.

'I don't know what – !'

'Now everybody quiet down,' Meg said.

The meetings were supposed to close on a positive note, so
after Complaints Olivia read us her latest poem, 'Sticks and
Stones.' *'Cunt, you call me,'* she began.

'Bag, bitch, piece of tail...'

After that the words ran, I heard them only as echoes.
When she finished, the meeting ended. I went to my room,
locked the door and fell back on the mattress. My chest hurt
and I thought I was having a heart attack. I lay there with my
arms crossed, pretending I was already dead.

Meg and I went shopping at the A&P: it was our turn to buy the weekly House Staples. I pushed the shopping cart while Meg read a list of groceries indexed alphabetically – JUICE, frozen; MILK, skim; TUNA, chunky, water-packed . . . We moved slowly, reading labels, checking prices along the way. With Gladys there was never time for dawdling. With Olivia extra minutes only increased the chance of her stashing something under her coat. But Meg was not a thief and in no particular hurry.

'So what flavor juice should we get, grapefruit or orange?'

'Grapefruit,' I said.

'The grapefruit's more expensive.'

'We always have orange. I'm tired of it.'

She paused to consider this. 'How about two grapefruit, two orange and skip the bag of noodles if we run short?'

I smiled at her, embarrassingly close to tears: that such a small gesture, such a little thing, could move me so.

'Now what about cereal? Raisin Bran?'

'Corn flakes.'

'Gladys likes Raisin Bran.'

I bumped the cart against a wall of boxes and they wobbled. 'Better get the bran then. Gladys will be so pleased.'

'I want to please you both if I can.'

'I know how special she is to you.'

Meg put a hand on the cart. 'Gladys is special to me, but why would I be mean to you because of that?'

I felt suddenly foolish. 'Get the Raisin Bran,' I said. 'It's okay.'

Later we broke the House Rules and splurged on something wonderful, vanilla fudge ice cream. It made me think of supermarket trips with Dad the years we lived together after Mother died. Filling carts with cans and boxes, finally vanilla fudge. It made me want to see him again – never mind about Helene.

🐚

I took the subway, train and bus to Dad and Helene's. They'd set up shop in an affluent suburb after a slump in Dad's business which he blamed on women's lib: 'Girls want to be hairy again, the eyebrows, armpits, even the legs. I haven't had a client under thirty-five in two years.' Helene, clean-shaven herself in all the usual places, found them a flat in a neighborhood where women still wore A-line dresses, pantyhose and spike heels and knew the worth of silky legs and armpits. Where only the poor immigrant who scrubbed your floors and made your beds had a hairy chin and upper lip. Business was good in Belmont County. Dad was booked solid, Monday to Saturday.

I arrived Sunday afternoon to find them both in the doorway, jostling for elbow room. Helene reached out and drew me close, but Dad pulled me away from her. 'Come to my office,' he said, 'I want to show you around.'

'No,' said Helene, tugging me back. 'She has to see the apartment first.'

Nice furniture, leather, chrome and glass, Scandinavian style. I sank into a canvas chair while Helene tiptoed across the rug, poking her head through a doorway. 'Okay, he's gone, we can talk now.' She lit up a cigarette and a plume of gray smoke rose above our heads. She peered at me. 'You look beat.'

'Group living wears you down. All those meetings eight to ten – some of them go even longer. After, I can never sleep.'

'It's no better here,' she said. 'Your father talks in his sleep, it drives me crazy. I'm tired all the time.'

'Maybe I'll move again.'

'You wouldn't like it out here – I don't. There's nothing to do. The younger wives go shopping and the older ones play mah-jongg. Your father works from morning to night, he's never around.' She walked a figure eight on the rug and waved the cigarette in the air. It made a smoky arc, a colorless rainbow. 'I'm still attractive,' said in a lower voice, 'I'm still young. I could try again.'

I sat up. 'You mean it?'

'Don't get so excited,' she said. 'I haven't made up my mind yet.'

Dad came into the room and batted my shoulder. 'That's enough. I waited long enough, get up.'

'Leave her alone,' Helene said.

Dad pulled me out of the chair and I followed him to his

office, bright with southern light. He sat down behind his desk, sallow-looking in the glare, and I had to squint to see his features, the thin nose and tight mouth. 'I'm worn out,' he said, and I almost laughed. 'Fifty-four and I feel like a hundred, know what I mean?'

'I know what you mean.' I sat on the edge of his huge desk and then, impulsively, leaned over and kissed his cheek. He blinked at me, his eyes wet.

All at once he clapped his hands and put his feet up on the desk. 'What can you do? At least business is booming here, the girls know what beauty is – skin like a baby's. No one's burning bras, no one's growing hair to their ankles.' His voice was hearty now. 'So, you like my office? Tell me the truth.'

Slowly I swung my head around. Everything was blurry in the watery light. 'Nice,' I whispered. 'Very nice.'

I was working in the typing pool of a glossy women's magazine when I got an invitation to a birthday party downtown. That was the night I met Sal. Salvatore Bianco. His name like bubbles popping as he put his lips against my ear and repeated it. We were stoned; we were dancing close. We moved like we were swimming in a fish tank. Later he wanted to take me home. But he'd left his keys in his jacket at his office across town. 'Too far to go,' he said. 'Let's go back to your place.'

'We can't.'

'Why not?'

'My roommates.'

He stopped dancing, lifted my chin and looked sternly into my eyes. 'I want you,' he said. 'I can't wait.'

I would've done anything he asked.

It was very late when we got to the apartment. We walked slowly, whispering and shushing, from the foyer to my bedroom, where we locked the door. I was trembling. 'Sssh, baby, sssh,' he said, stroking me, kissing me. 'Just relax, we've got all night.'

All night in Sal's arms. So excited I couldn't breathe. Listening to Sal's breath, in, out, in and out, slow at first, then speeding up. Faster, faster – one-two, one-two – and I was doing it too, I was feeling it too, one-one, two-two, now now now *yes!*

Sal, my sweet, my one-and-only fuzzy-wuzzy big bear.

In the morning he was gone before I heard anyone moving about, but at breakfast they were waiting for me. 'Who did you bring home last night?' Gladys asked.

'That *man*,' Olivia jumped in.

'It's really none of your business.'

'He could've been a Charles Manson,' Olivia said. 'He could've stabbed us in our sleep!'

'He's someone I met at a party. A nice guy.'

At the next Thursday House Meeting Gladys and Olivia complained about me – the nerve of me sneaking a man, a stranger, into my room and not telling anyone what I was up to. 'I never slept the whole night,' Gladys announced. 'I was terrified,' Olivia cried. Even Meg said, 'Me too.' They accused me of choosing subjugation over sisterhood, patriarchy over freedom.

I was struck dumb, my macramé unraveling, hanging from my lap in loops. I snatched the string and squeezed it into small lumps. They were watching me. They were waiting. 'It won't happen again,' I said. 'I didn't know.'

'There,' said Meg, 'she didn't know. We have to give her another chance.'

'She's always saying "I don't know,"' Olivia said. 'She ought to know something by now.'

'High time she learned the rules,' Gladys agreed.

Then Olivia read a poem, 'What I See with My Speculum.'

🧠

'They're telling you how to live your life,' Sal said. '"No men allowed." You want to be free – great! – but do it your own way, your own rules. Liberation is choice, doing what you choose.'

'I can't seem to please them,' I said.

'Hell,' he said, 'you please me.' He cupped my face in his hands and kissed me deeply. 'Why not come live with me? No meetings, no hassles and all the sex you can handle.'

'Sounds good.'

It was New Year's Eve. We were sitting in Sal's living room in front of a small fireplace where a fake log was burning down to a puddle of wax. We were drinking California wine and listening to Guy Lombardo's orchestra on the radio.

'Make a resolution,' he said. 'Move in with me and look for a real job.'

'What do you mean, "a real job"?'

'You need a career – a goal – something to strive for. You can't work those office jobs till you drop dead.'

'Why not?'

'It's no life.'

I inched away from him. 'What's so great about your life? You tell women how to invest and they run your column between an ad for Tampax and a spread on Funky Hair-dos for Fall.'

'It's not so much what you're doing now but what you aspire to that counts. In a few years I expect to be a well-respected journalist writing political exposés.' He hugged his knees and gazed at the ceiling, awed by his dream.

'I don't think that far in advance.'

But Sal was already at the window, peering down, where even at this late hour trucks and buses rumbled by. He pressed his palms against the rattling panes of glass. 'Everyone will know my name . . . movers and shakers, shopkeepers, newsboys . . .'

In twenty minutes it would be 1972. The year stretched before me like the line of traffic outside, bright and loud, a blur of shapes that never slowed. Frightening to join that flow but safe enough to watch from here, ten stories high. Olivia, Meg and Gladys wouldn't understand. They'd say that I was giving up, moving in with the enemy, but I saw it a different way: I needed space.

❀

After work and on days off I read, sewed or sketched a bit, and twice a week I studied yoga with Mrs. Craig, a muscular woman who taught class in black fishnet stockings and a leotard. She had a deep, commanding voice which I followed through several contortions, through head stands and shoulder stands, bow, locust, cobra, plow. There were eight regulars in our class, and though sometimes we'd nod at each other we never spoke but concentrated on our twists as Mrs. Craig stepped among us, correcting our posture – here a neck that needed straightening, there a spine. When she pressed the heels of her hands into my back and shoulders or turned my head, I was deeply moved. It wasn't sexual – something else – something I called a 'mystical experience.'

My favorite pose was deep relaxation. We would lie on mats with our eyes closed, trying to relax our bodies and empty our minds while Mrs. Craig chanted, 'The back of your head is heavy and broad, your neck is broad, the shoulders are broad, your eyeballs loose in their sockets and your jaw is loose, the tongue is soft . . .' We would focus on a calm image – water slapping against a shore, a seagull on a lamp-post or a grain of sand – everything illuminated by white light. A blank space, a hole in time, a place to enter and rest in . . . Onlyville. Standing in the muslin fog, waiting for the *Island Queen*: a wrap of stillness, pillow of fog, a world on the edge of sleep. But then a rush, a white shape – white ship – and Mother calling from the deck. I strain to catch her words but I can't hear them through the fog, everything distorted, and my body tenses suddenly, I roll against the thick fog. Then I'm on the floor again, restless and cold, Mrs. Craig instructing us to sit up now, half lotus, breathe deeply, pull those stomach muscles in, expand the chest . . .

At home in Sal's apartment I practiced yoga every day but couldn't relax with the radio playing, the typewriter clacking and him talking. All that noise. 'You ought to study politics,' he told me one evening as he kicked a book of adult education courses across the floor. 'Tune in to the real world. Nixon's bombing Cambodia and you're standing on your head.'

'Take care of your own life,' I answered in a squelched voice. From upside down he looked like a man with a wavy beard, a fringe of hair and a gaping eye in his forehead.

'I worry about you, that's all. I mean, if you hadn't run into me who knows where you'd be right now. Out on the street.'

'I can look after myself,' I said, and then I toppled over.

❀

The weekend I turned twenty-eight he rented a car and reserved a room in a country inn. We set out early Saturday when the sun was low and traffic light. Just beyond the city limits trees shimmied red and gold and the air was October-fresh. I rolled the passenger window down and caught a sweet whiff of decay. Sal was busy changing lanes and tailing leisurely drivers. To him the point of traveling was to get somewhere as fast as you could, turn around and come back.

'Take a deep breath,' I said.

'Don't give me that deep relaxation shit.'

'I only meant for you to breathe some country air.'

'Damn potheads can't stay in the lane,' he said, weaving around a psychedelically painted van.

When we got to the inn our room was small, though nicely furnished with antiques and a canopied bed. Sal wanted something bigger but nothing else was available. He wanted to leave but I pleaded, 'It's my birthday, I like it here,' so we unpacked. He rolled a couple of joints and said, 'Let's go find the bar.'

The lounge was jammed with young men in blue tuxedoes and women in purple taffeta gowns sitting around a fireplace where a log smoldered and flared into peaks. Sal ordered a pitcher of beer and we sat at the bar, watching the pink faces of the members of the wedding party, hearing the murmur of conversation, of stockinged legs rubbed together and yards of swishing fabric. And I wished I was one of those giggling bridesmaids dreaming of catching the bride's bouquet, in love with a sweet-eyed usher, the names of my children-to-be already decided.

Sal loped off to the washroom, coming back with the heavy smell of marijuana on his clothes. He drew his bar stool up to mine and pressed his lips against my ear. 'I know what you're thinking,' he said, 'you want to get married.' He brushed my cheek with his moustache. 'You want to marry, I'll marry you. I'll take care of you always.'

'I don't want you taking care of me – okay?' My voice mean, surprising me. 'I won't marry anyone!' I shouted, and charged out.

I crossed the road to a dirt path and turned sharply into the woods. It was darker here, the light dim. Leaves crackled, branches snapped as I ran from one field to the next, through oaks, birches, evergreens, and over a hill, an old bridge, a stone wall. On the other side of the wall I stopped – panting, sweaty, light-headed – coldness under my hot cheeks. What if a band of hunters – ? Or a wounded bear.

I climbed a ridge, looked around, but nothing was familiar, and not even a shack in sight. I faced the sun, the sun sinking – that was west. Yes, west. The inn was east – northeast. No, south. Southeast. I spun round and round like the needle of a compass gone wild.

Lost. I'm lost.

Not lost.

I'm lost, I'm lost!

I started running toward a stream I'd seen before – hadn't seen – *did see!* – the voices in my head screaming, *Right! Left! Stay where you are!* Tripping on a root, I fell, and my jeans darkened around the knees. I rolled back, landing in mud, and cried like an abandoned child.

Sal found me before dark, dirty and bloody beside a tree not very far from the road. He tied his jacket around my shoulders, scooped me to his chest and squeezed. 'Never run away like that again, it's too dangerous. You could've gotten lost for good.'

'I didn't mean to get lost.' My voice so small and quivery it made me feel weepy again.

'I hope you're sorry,' Sal said, kissing my eyes.

He smelled of smoke and too much beer, his moustache was sticky and his eyes red. But soon he would bathe me, buy me dinner, give me a nice birthday gift and stroke me to forgetfulness on a canopied bed. Soon, in spite of everything – in spite of every damn thing! – I'd fall asleep, grateful and sorry, in Sal's arms.

❦

In spring, when the city breathed out warm air, I felt dead. Daily I followed different streets to different buildings with marble lobbies and shiny mirrored elevators to sit at desks and do things I had no recollection of by evening. Every morning I looked forward to being in bed again, fast asleep.

Sal said, 'What's wrong? You're turning into a zombie.' I didn't know how to answer. I didn't want to think about it, I wanted to sleep.

Finally it was a bud on a young maple tree that stirred me, a tree in one of those concrete planters set on city streets at regular intervals. A tree with roots contained in a tub and not allowed to spread beneath the sidewalk: a guarded tree. Around its trunk, butts and paper, cans and gum, its branches drooping under a weight of dirty air. Yet it pushed forth a bud, green and delicate, tightly wrapped, wet with life.

I can't recall the street I was on or which job I was going to, but I clearly remember that single bud and how it stopped me in my tracks and startled me alert again and how, with sudden energy, I bought a paper, made some calls and rented an apartment that very day. I packed my bags and left Sal.

My two-room semi-basement was noisy and dark. The upstairs neighbor played drums, the buzzer on the door to the building rang often, ferociously, and the frequent slamming of that door rearranged my furniture by inches. There were roaches too, a band that scampered under the door and didn't bother fleeing when I crossed their paths. At night I dreamed about them climbing up the bed and over me; I felt their legs and long antennae and woke sweating, slapping my face.

One such night I phoned Jay. I had to talk to someone and it couldn't be Sal. Margot answered, yawning loudly into the phone.

'Is Jay home?'

'No.'

'When will he be in?'

'Don't know. What'd you want to ask him?'

'Oh, nothing much,' I said, keeping my voice cheerful. 'Just wanted to say hello. I haven't called in ages.'

'The store's doing great,' she said. 'Everyone's into vitamins and granola.'

'And you?'

'Well, I miss snow.'

'How're you liking grade . . .' What? I couldn't think.

'Grade eight. It's okay.'

The receiver crackled. I stared at the cord that ran to the jack: wires strung from here to there, cables going underground to a distant coast. How far away Margot was. How little she could do to help.

Margot said, 'I have to go. I'll tell Dad you called,' and the line went dead.

Back in bed I lay still and unthinking, eyes closed, and breathed deeply, in and out. I focused on an image of snow: the doors of the house in Regency Hills welded shut by fallen snow; snow on the roof, in the eavestroughs, in the corners of the window panes. Margot and I indoors, safe and warm.

In the morning I woke stiff and tired and went to work in the typing pool of a large corporation, my fingers stuck to an Olivetti, my face gray as that big machine. In the cafeteria other typists and secretaries, a tide of women in tight dresses, jostled for seats around a table. I sat among them, inattentive, their words clicking in my ears: the one-syllable names of men (Ben, Bob, John and Jim), the names of Club Med villages (Martinique and Guadeloupe), the names of diets (Pritikin, Scarsdale, Grapefruit).

&

An ad in the paper read, 'Change your life through ENCOUNTER. Experience heightened awareness and get in touch with your feelings in a group marathon workshop.' It took days to make up my mind, but then I phoned.

The leader's name was Les Payne. I saw that as a good omen. Thirteen of us met in his apartment in a neighborhood known for artists' lofts and funky shops. We flopped down on cushions on a cold floor. The ceiling was scored with track lighting, one bulb aimed at Les, who sat higher than us on a beach chair in a cone of light. A thirtyish man with a wide face, his hair tied in a ponytail, wearing a snug T-shirt with the message *CELF: Center for Emotional Fulfillment*.

'Let's go round the room,' he said, 'and everyone say a little bit about yourself, what's on your mind, why you're here.'

Six men and women spoke, using words like 'sensitivity,'

'mind-fuck' and 'relating,' while others said encouragingly, 'Dynamite!' and 'Out of sight!' Les bent forward, listening.

It was my turn. 'My name's Anna,' I said, 'and I don't know what I'm doing here.'

Les' neck extended and he shortened the distance between us. 'You know why you're here,' he said.

'No, really.'

'Bullshit!' He snapped to his feet and stood over me, narrow-eyed. I leaned back on an elbow, presenting him with my right flank.

'All of a sudden you don't want to be here, right? You're sorry you came. You thought it would be easy, huh? – pay your money at the door and change your life. All you got to do is lis-ten – no work and no responsibility!' He stepped back and eyed the others. 'Isn't that what you *all* want? You want me to tell you how to fix your sad little lives, one-two-three. Because you can't do anything yourselves, you're such a sorry bunch.' He waved the back of his hand in disgust at those who hadn't yet introduced themselves. 'I don't want to hear from you, you're all alike. Boring. You make me sick.'

Then he took his seat again and closed his eyes. His head lolled forward and he slumped in the chair. He began to snore. We glanced at each other, looked away, squirmed on our cush-ions, this way and that, waiting for Les to wake up. Ten min-utes later he came to and clapped his hands. 'Everyone up! Take off your shoes. That's right, don't panic, just your shoes. We're going to do some exercises, help you get to know each other. Increase your awareness.'

We pulled off our shoes and stood up. A young man held a pair of cowboy boots against his chest. 'Put them down,' Les said. He moved closer to the man, and I thought he would snatch the boots away. Instead he dropped down in front of two women, scooping the left foot of one and the right foot of the other into his big hands. The women fought for balance as he gently massaged their feet.

He rose to his full height. 'See what I did, I spoke to them, got to know them, *made contact*, without saying a single word. Now I want all of you to do the same. Walk around and check each other out with your eyes. Stop in front of someone interesting, look at them closely, no talking. Get to know them with your fingers. What are they saying to your hands?'

A man stopped in front of me and studied my eyes, his mouth turning serious. He had the look of a child playing grownup and I almost laughed. He patted my face – that was fine – but then his fingers ran down my neck and across my breasts. Go away! I stared back at him. How dare you – stop that! He put a finger over his lips and moved on.

Later there was arm-wrestling, non-verbal confrontation and falling backward into someone's waiting arms. In another game we lifted a person over our heads, rocked him back and forth and set him down again. After a lunch of herbal tea and sandwiches we lay down on folded blankets side by side. 'Close your eyes,' Les instructed, 'we're going to take a body trip. Imagine yourself getting smaller and smaller . . . microscopic. Now enter your body anywhere you like and have a look around. Travel through your blood vessels, visit your ears, your heart and lungs, your guts, your groin, wherever you want.'

I shrank to the size of a pinhead and ducked under an eyelid. I swam around my eyeball, alarmed by the total darkness, then swung from nerve to nerve to my brain. I rolled among the gray swells, like bouncing on a waterbed, and struck a lump as small as a pea. When I pushed it my body jackknifed, and I was thrown against my skull.

Les was clapping, 'Everyone up! Open your eyes. Tell us about your fantasy.'

People had traveled to guts and genitals, kidneys and spleens. They described scenes like those in *Fantastic Voyage*: propelled by a heartbeat, whirled by a breath, attacked by giant phagocytes. Throughout these recitations there were murmurs of 'Beautiful!' 'Far out!' and 'Fuckin' wild!'

'And you?' Les was pointing at me. Everyone hushed: a sudden ragged silence.

'I visited my brain,' I said.

'What did you find?'

'A headache.'

He squatted on my blanket – we were inches apart – and pressed his fingers on my temples. 'Talk to your headache,' he commanded, 'out loud.'

'Headache, go away,' I said.

'No, no!' He pushed his fingers deeper into my forehead. 'Ask your headache why it's happening, what does it want?'

'Anacin.'

He locked my jaw shut in his hands. 'No more talking – not a word! Now you're going to feel something . . . just feel.'

He loosened his grip and my jaw fell. He jammed his mouth against mine as we stared into each other's eyes. I hardly paid attention to the urgent goings-on in my mouth, that jabbing tongue, those slippery lips. What mattered was to look deeply into his eyes and find something striking there, yellow light. To enter it and feel its warmth. To be sunny, filled with light.

Only blackness in his eyes, nothing more. I felt that I was drowning in a black sea. No one here would rescue me – everybody for himself.

I ran to the door and downstairs. Outside it was drizzling and the streets were gray. I dropped my head between my knees, the air so thick I couldn't seem to draw it in. What if I fainted dead away? Keeled over head first and lay in the gutter, arms wide? Surely someone would save me then.

Sal was by the window. No radio played, no TV, and even the drill and rattle of the street was muted, far away. He gazed from my duffel bag, humped on the floor, up to my face, down to my feet. There were dark patches under his eyes and shadows under his cheekbones. I said, 'Am I welcome?'

He turned to the window, and I felt a wavering in my legs. Then he crossed the room to the door and bent low to hug me. His back shivered under my hands. I pulled him to the sofa and eased his head onto my lap. His eyes were squeezed tightly shut and he breathed rapidly through his mouth. Suddenly he cried out, not an intelligible word but the raw note that sometimes tumbles out of a dream, and he kissed my thigh under my skirt.

We dropped to the floor and shook off our clothes. We pressed together without pause or tenderness, like something out of a movie. But when we awoke from the daze of our love-making, things became familiar at once. Sal smoked the stub of a joint, then turned on the radio: 'Vice President Spiro Agnew has resigned ...'

He crouched in front of the radio and motioned me close. 'We'll have to listen carefully and take notes. Keep a list of who's who and everything that's happening.' He slapped a hand on my shoulder. '"The Nixon Years and the End of Innocence" – how's that? Or maybe something bolder like "Death of the Democratic System."'

'The good guys are winning,' I said.

'"Triumph of the Democratic System" then.' He snatched the radio. 'Come here.'

In the bedroom he waved me into a chair, turned up the radio and tossed a pack of newspapers onto my lap. 'Read these.' Then he sat down at his desk, fingers on the typewriter keys. Bam-bam-bam, the keys played their monotonous song. I opened a paper and read the headline, RICHARDSON AND RUCKELSHAUS RESIGN.

'Listen to this,' he said. 'When the Weathermen exploded in New York in 1970, when Jimi Hendrix and Janis Joplin overdosed that same year and National Guardsmen fired at the student movement at Kent State, the counter-culture ran for cover – and with it a voice, however shrill, raised against the excesses of government was silenced.'

'Sounds great,' I said proudly.

'Now, as Nixon's administration unravels and its dirty secrets are revealed, we're seeing just how unbridled that government is.'

'Keep going,' I goaded him as sheet after sheet of rumpled paper shot from his fist, as the typewriter stopped and started in thunderclaps. I sat there with my hands clenched, papers jiggling on my lap, and thought, Do it, don't stop!

All afternoon and evening and the next day, I listened to the radio, read papers and urged him on. If I left the room for a minute Sal would follow me and coax me back, 'I can't do it without you, you're my good luck.' In the dizziness of that weekend I believed him, believed that by my presence I could change him; that when at last he wrote his essay something would change in me too.

He never finished his article. Oh, there were reasons, of

course – layoffs at the magazine that increased his workload, an argument with the editor that made him look for a new job (an ordeal which finally sent him running back to his old one). Once he came home drunk from an interview and collapsed on the couch. 'So I said, "Hey, you know how many years I been doing this?" and he said, "That's the trouble, Sal . . . Sal, m'boy, the trouble is . . . " I know what he meant, the cock-sucker . . . burned out, pfft! like I'm no good for anything . . .'

He wasn't talking to me, he was just talking, slurring words, repeating himself. I sat and listened, the evening paper on my lap. Maybe he would sober up and – do what? Read the paper? Finish his article? Write a book? Soon I began to hate his voice, that march of words that went nowhere, solved nothing. Why did I ever think he was capable of greatness?

Later he heaved himself off the sofa, eyes veined and unfocused, and stumbled toward me. 'Coffee?' I asked. He blinked, rolled back on his heels and lifted an arm. I tensed, eyes fixed on his hand. He swung forward and swatted the paper off my knees.

'I was reading something interesting,' I told him, 'about the eighteen-minute gap in Nixon's tape.'

He threw back his head and wailed, a sound so full of pain I had to cover my ears. Then he reeled into the bedroom, lock-ing the door behind him.

That winter it snowed as it hadn't in years. Snow piled up on window sills and covered the glass in curlicues. A muted city, sluggish and cold. Cars crept through brown slush like bears shaken from hibernation too soon. On the bus to work, on the bus home, the smell of wet wool and hair, of mentholated cough drops.

If it hadn't snowed I might have left in December, a tidy wrap-up to the year. In January, time for new beginnings, or in February, when week after week of gray skies dulls your vision, then your soul, and every part of you cries for change. But it snowed hard those three months and how could I look for somewhere to live with ice on my boots weighing me down, with snow sealing doorways shut and falling from roofs?

All that time I came and went, as Sal came and went too. At night I skimmed the papers while in another room, behind a closed and locked door, the typewriter tapped and the radio played faintly. My thoughts ran free then, like sand through a fist. Green thoughts, crimson thoughts; thoughts of water, sun and grass. I could almost hear the ferry whistle and feel mist on my eyelids.

I chose the beginning of April to leave, when crocuses sprouted in window boxes and streets were loamy-smelling with the new season, when tree limbs were ragged with buds, and Sal was out. I left a note on the radio: 'Goodbye again, for good this time. Don't look for me, I want to live alone.'

I carried my duffel bag on my back and called the doorman up to help me with the rest. Then I was in a taxi heading downtown to the train station, on my way to Onlyville. I stared out the window spattered with mud, my view distorted. Everything broken into fragments, turning, falling, changing, like the bits of colored glass in a kaleidoscope. 'Hurry up,' I told the driver. 'Hurry, please.'

FOUR: 1974

I WAKE AT TWO in the morning with an ache in my chest and I roll over, slamming into a block of flesh. Sal, I remember suddenly. Sal, Neil and Margot. I close my eyes and try to recapture a dream I was having about Dad: Dad on the beach in Onlyville, wearing a suit and carrying a briefcase. Something leaking from the case, staining the sand with dark coins. He hears the dripping and looks back, sees the long trail of spots, falls to his knees and opens the case. Inside is a beating heart. 'Oh my God!' he cries out. He shoves a hand under his shirt and it goes through a hole in his chest, his fingers fluttering in the air like the feathers of a frightened bird.

I interpret my dream to mean that Dad is having a heart attack. Right now. I pull on my kimono and hurry to The Boulevard, into the phone booth grainy in the light of the moon.

Helene answers, bushy-voiced: 'Who? Anna? What's the matter? This some kind of emergency? Where are you?'

'In Onlyville.'

'What? What're you doing there? Why are you calling so late – are you sick? In some kind of trouble?'

'It's about Dad. Is he all right?'

'Certainly. You having a bad trip?'

'Can I speak to him?'

'Maybe there's something I can do.'

'I need to talk to my father.'

When he gets on the line I ask him if he's okay. 'Sure I'm okay,' he says. 'Why shouldn't I be?'

'I had this dream about you, about your heart. I was worried.'

'Well, it's nice to know you think of me once in a while, even at two in the morning. Nice of you to wonder if I'm still alive.'

'It was so real,' I try again. 'I thought you were having a heart attack.'

'Every now and then I get a few pains. I try not to pay attention. I think maybe it's gas and I have a drink of water.'

'Does that help?'

'Sometimes. But sometimes it stays with me, I can't sleep.'

'Have you seen a doctor?'

'No, no. I lie there till it goes away. You can get used to anything, even pain. But not tonight – tonight I'm feeling okay.'

'*My* chest is hurting tonight.'

'At your age it's gas for sure, nothing to get upset about. Don't think about it now, go back to bed. Tomorrow you'll feel better, you can call again and we'll talk more. But now I'm tired, it's too late.'

In the cottage again, back in bed, I listen to Sal moan in his sleep. 'Sal?' I whisper. 'You awake?'

'Die,' he grunts, 'die!' as his hands twist the phantom neck of a North Korean sniper.

I go to the kitchen and make tea, then ease into the rocking chair, resting my cup on one of its arms. From there I can see through a window into the starry night, past the shadows of stunted trees and into the room of another house: a room, a light, some furniture. I picture a woman sitting there and reach out to touch her, but her image breaks into bubbles.

In the morning my eyes are crusted shut, my body doubled over in the rocking chair. The song of birds is loud and shrill. I stand and rub my eyes open, walk around. No one downstairs yet, the rooms neither dark nor light, but someone dancing on the deck – Neil, Margot's strange friend. Not really dancing, doing tai chi, rhythmical and graceful, the slow movements drawing me to the patio doors. The screen door wobbles as I open it, and he twists around to face me, swinging his hips and shoulders, crossing and uncrossing his arms. When he straightens up our eyes meet, and I hold his look. I lean forward and touch his hand, the knuckles cool and delicate. He neither draws his hand away nor offers it and after a moment, warm with growing embarrassment, I pull back.

I go to the Singer and start sewing, the needle poking in and out of the cloth with the sound of kissing. May already – so much to be done. So many distractions. Neil comes in, his shadow passing in front of me, but I don't look up. Soon I hear the recorder. Then the radio, turned up loud, and the eight o'clock news: 'Today the House Judiciary starts hearing evidence as part of its impeachment investigation . . .'

Concentrate, I tell myself. *Keep going.*

'Awright!' Sal hollers from the stairs. 'They're closing in on the bastard.' He sits down across from me and starts banging the typewriter keys. He doesn't stop when Margot bounds into the room, but I do. She's barefoot, wearing a slight bikini, carrying a small plaid makeup bag. There's more cloth in the bag than in her entire suit. She flops down on the sofa beside Neil, pulls a compact from the bag and lays it open on her thigh. Holding mascara, she hunches over the mirror and begins painting her lashes.

'What're you doing?' I say.

'My eyes. Cover Girl – it's waterproof.' She zips closed the makeup bag and jumps up. 'Who's going swimming?' she asks.

Neil shakes his head and I remind her that I can't swim.

'Still? You never learned how? I can't believe it – living here and you can't swim.' She sticks her hip out at Sal. 'And you? Will you come swimming with me?'

'Got to work,' Sal says.

She walks up to the typewriter and looks over his shoulder. 'What's it about?'

He yanks a sheet from the roller and reads aloud. 'He told us he wanted "to do the right thing," so last week President Nixon made public more than a thousand pages of Watergate conversations. Though many subpoenaed tapes were not among these transcripts and much of what was handed over was edited, the conversations show him reacting to the burglary determined not to uphold the law but to limit the investigations and consequences of the act. Rather than seek to reveal the truth, Nixon struggled "to keep the cap on the bottle" and to "tough it through."'

Sal rolls the sheet back. Margot rubs a pieced-together jumper lying by the Singer, humming something under her breath. Sal says, 'That's the opening paragraph.' He seems to be speaking to all of us. 'Do you like it?'

Neil blows a note on his recorder. Margot says, 'Don't know much about politics,' and starts singing Carole King.

Sal looks at me. 'What do you think?'

'Interesting.'

'*Interesting* – what does that mean?' He slaps the paper, 'No good, that's what you mean,' and slumps in his seat.

Go to him, I'm thinking. *Tell him it's really good. Encourage him.*

I back away from the table, and Sal looks up expectantly. Then, to my surprise, I tear off to the beach. Along the shore, in the wet sand, I start running full stride. Speeding toward the horizon where a body can circle the edge of the world, never stopping, never meeting anyone.

The house on Blueberry falls behind, then I can't see it at all. I let out a whoop. Someone answers my shout and I stop in my tracks to look around. Here and there the beach is dotted with sunbathers, no one I know. Suddenly I hear my name – 'Anna, wait!' – and Margot bounds into me. 'Thought I'd never catch you,' she puffs.

She drops to the sand, pulling me down, and swings her head onto my lap. 'Oh!' I say and shut my eyes, remembering the afternoon Bonnie showed up at the bungalow and braided Margot's hair with a casualness and certainty about her young daughter's love that amazed me. I open my eyes. Slowly I lower my hand onto Margot's head and work my fingers into her hair.

'I was thinking about my mother,' she says, 'this famous skater she works for. She's like her private secretary, taking care of things when they're on the road. They get to travel everywhere, the whole world.'

'I know she likes to travel but she must get lonely sometimes, and homesick.'

'She sent me a clipping from Europe once. The skater won a medal in the championships.'

'Do you see her at all?'

'She doesn't get to the Coast much, but when she does, sure I do. We meet for dinner in nice places, not cheap. She brings me presents too,' her voice faltering. Then she sits up. 'Let's go back now.'

We follow our tracks past the old rickety house on the edge of town, a place I used to think was haunted by dead slaves and buccaneers. Something eerie about it still, abandoned.

Margot shoves me. 'Don't you care what I want to be when I'm older? I mean, you haven't asked yet.'

'Okay, what?'

'An actress. My mother thinks it's a good idea. I've got my

eye on one of those little white apartments all in a row with a pool in the yard. If you're pretty enough you meet people, no trouble. First you get some photos done and take them around. Then while you're waiting to get discovered you find a job – cocktail waitress, something like that – and make some friends that're looking for a break too. You hang around the pool sometimes and maybe go to drive-ins, but mostly you're busy working nights and doing auditions all day.'

'Hollywood's not what it used to be. You'll wind up in a porno film if you get in front of a camera at all.'

'You sound like Dad,' Margot says, 'always thinking the worst. I guess you want me to sell alfalfa sprouts like him.'

'I don't know – of course not – whatever you want,' but Margot races ahead of me, her attention already shifted, and I'm worried I said the wrong thing.

Down the beach she crouches by a dark figure in the sand with his knees pulled up and his back humped. The young man from the Mini-Mart, I see as I come near, the surly clerk in green fatigues. I stop just in front of them, and he cups a hand over his eyes and looks up. I stand stiff, like a child caught doing something naughty.

He grunts at Margot and lowers his head. She says, 'He wants to be alone.'

'So let's go.'

'He doesn't mean me,' she says. 'I'll catch up to you later.'

'Oh. Well.' I turn toward the house again, a tick starting between my eyes.

Back at the cottage Sal is on the chaise longue, drinking beer. Neil is sitting across the deck, reading a Carlos Castaneda paperback.

I wrinkle my nose at Sal. 'Beer in the morning?'

'Helps me think.'

'How's your essay going?'

'What do you care?'

I straddle the front rail of the deck. The tick between my eyes is now a hard beat. Neil walks up to me, gazing at his open book. 'Listen,' he says, 'you'll like this. "Any path is only a path," ' he quotes the sorcerer Don Juan. 'That means if you don't feel like going a certain way, you don't have to. Think about it.' He closes the book and hands it to me – 'Here, a gift' – then heads off toward the beach. I watch him till he disappears behind the dunes, and it seems to me he leaves a trail of shimmering air.

Sal says, 'One helluva weird kid.'

'Oh shut up!'

I go upstairs and lie down in the back room. I don't remember falling asleep but the light in the room is suddenly changed and Margot's at the foot of the bed, speaking to me. 'That guy on the beach,' she says, 'the one I was talking to – you know, the one in Army clothes? He wasn't in the Army at all, he was 4F. Because of his knee, he says, this torn cartilage. Some guys do that deliberately, they go and get their knees cut up, but I don't think that happened to him. I think he wanted to go to Nam and shoot gooks. I think he's nuts – for real, I mean – that's why they gave him 4F.' She bites her lip. 'I think it's kind of sad,' she says. 'Underneath he's a nice guy.'

It rains a lot the rest of the month and into June. The spattering on the roof and deck is soothing at first, but then becomes monotonous. Neil is gone most of the time, staying out overnight with his tent and a sleeping bag, exploring parts of the island. First he studies the old map on the living room wall, then we don't see him for days.

Sal and I stay indoors. I get a little sewing done but he doesn't write his article. He drinks beer, an ear cocked to the radio. The Vietnam War is old news but Watergate is hotter than ever. In mid-June Nixon's lawyer gets six to eighteen months in jail, then Colson one to three years. Though he listens, Sal is unenthused. Food becomes his passion and he cooks lots of dinners for us – stuffed bass, sole florentine, chicken in cream. We gain weight.

Margot is bored but doesn't want to do anything. She doesn't want to hike with Neil, cook with Sal, read or sew. She only speaks to me to complain. 'How can you sit there cutting and stitching? Doesn't it drive you crazy, such a nothing job? When're you gonna sell this stuff anyway?' Or, 'How can you stand being here? It's not so bad on weekends when there's people around, but all the rest of the time it's like a graveyard.'

Then she charges outside, on her way to the store or the dock.

When the rain lets up and the beach fills, when boats cruise the bay again and the air smells of barbecues, Margot leaves in the morning and doesn't come back till suppertime. Evenings she slips out again – with Neil if he's around but mostly on her own – and doesn't turn up till eleven. 'Where does she go?' Sal asks. 'How can you let her wander around in the dark like that?'

'She can take care of herself,' I say.

But one Friday night she isn't home till two. When I hear her in the kitchen I race down in my nightgown, switching on lights as I cross the room. I find her on the couch, eating a bag of chips, her face pale and woozy.

'Since when do you stay out so late? Where were you?'

'Oh, around … the dock, the bay.'

'Mosquitoes would've eaten you alive by now.'

'They did!' she giggles, pulling up her sweatshirt to reveal a line of red bumps.

'Who were you with?'

She waves a hand. 'Different people.'

'What people?'

'No one you know. There was a party … one of the houses on the bay.'

'Which house?'

'The one with the red door, you know?'

'I don't know, and I can't believe you crashed some party …'

'I was *asked*.'

'And never said a word to me.'

'I wasn't sure I wanted to go.'

'So you got drunk –'

'I didn't drink.'

'– and got stoned.'

'Nothing wrong with a little weed.'

'And did whatever else you did.'

'You're not my mother,' Margot says. 'You can't tell me what to do.'

'You're my guest,' I say, stiffening. 'I don't have to put up with this.'

'My father owns this house too, it's not just yours. I have a right to be here if I want to.'

'I'm phoning him tomorrow and we'll see about that.'

'Go ahead.' She trails up to the front room, kicking the door behind her.

Then I stomp upstairs too, hurling my own door shut. Sal wakes up. 'What's going on?'

I lie down and elbow him on the mattress. 'Move over, you're hogging the bed.'

'If I move any more I'll fall off. What do you want, the whole bed?'

I sit up straight. 'As a matter of fact that's just what I want, the whole bed. I want you to leave, the sooner the better. I don't have to put up with either one of you!'

He looks confused. 'You're tired,' he says. 'Go back to sleep.'

'I want you out. I said I wanted to live alone and I mean it.'

'You don't know what you want.' He shifts onto his left side and pulls the blanket over his head.

I pound his back with my fists. 'Get up! Get out of here!'

'For chrissake!' He throws off the covers, swings to his feet and finds his suitcase under the bed. He makes a show of filling it, scooping underwear out of drawers, snapping shirts and pants from hangers, shooting everything into the case. 'I've had enough of you too,' he snarls at me from the doorway.

'Don't forget your radio. It's on the fridge.'

When I hear the front door slam I let out a breath. My pulse is doing double time. I stretch out on the empty bed but can't fall asleep again. Hours later I must have dozed off because I'm suddenly shocked by a ferry whistle: the ten o'clock boat. Bye-bye Sal. I roll out of bed and go downstairs but stop short at the bottom step. Sal is on the living room couch, curled on his side with his eyes closed, his hands squeezed between his knees.

I phone Jay at his food store, the Rising Sun. 'It's not working out,' I say. 'She's bored here, she ought to go.'

'She wants to?'

'*I* think it's a good idea.'

'What about Neil?' Jay asks.

'He's off on his own most of the time.'

'That's a relief.'

'Neil's a good influence on Margot, if you ask me.'

'Look,' he says at last, 'I've thought a lot about this. She's better off with you, at least for the summer. We're not getting along right now, she doesn't like my girlfriend.'

'I don't care about all that. I came here to be alone, now I'm lining up to get in the bathroom.'

'Anna, please,' his voice softening. 'Margot needs to be with you.'

'She needs to be with you too.'

'I'll send a check to cover her expenses.'

'You're missing the point.'

'Do me a favor and think about it, try to get along with her. We're not talking a lifetime, just two months. That'll give me time to settle a few things. Okay? Will you help me out?'

'I'll think about it.'

'Good,' he says. 'We'll be in touch.'

Neil is on the roof hammering, bare-chested and gleaming. 'What're you doing?' I shout up at him.

'Fixing the roof,' he says. 'It leaks.'

A ladder leans against the house, wedged between the boardwalk and eavestrough. At the foot of it are coiled rope, cans of tar, boxes of shingles and roofing nails. 'Where did you get all this?' I ask.

His arm stops in mid-arc – 'Borrowed some, bought some' – then he slams the hammer against a nail.

Margot appears in a T-shirt and the bottom half of a striped bikini, standing shoulder to shoulder with me, watching Neil. 'Hey, he's on the roof,' she says.

'You know where all this came from?'

'That hardware store in the Cove. They sent it by boat.'

'Neil paid?'

She clicks her tongue. 'He works, you know – carpentry, painting, roofing too – whatever people need done.'

'How much does he charge?'

'He's not going to *charge* you. This is how he says thanks.'

'Oh,' my cheeks tingling. 'I mean, I hardly know him and your father doesn't trust him at all.'

'You spoke to Dad?'

'This morning.'

Margot stares down at her toes, trying to spread them yoga-style. 'So when's he coming to get me?'

'It's up to me, whether or not I want you around.'

She wiggles her toes, 'I won't stay out late anymore,' and twists the hem of her T-shirt into a knot. 'I like it here,' a pause, 'with you. Don't send me home, okay?'

Something in her voice like Jay's – that mix of toughness and pleading – softens me. 'We'll try to get along,' I say, 'and see how it goes.'

Neil calls, 'Margot, tie that rope to a can and pass me the other end,' and she hurries to the ladder. Sal comes out and leans against a deck rail, drinking beer from the bottle. He watches Neil on the slope of the roof pull a rope hand over hand and says, 'What the hell's going on?'

I ignore him.

'You're not talking? The silent treatment? That's the way it's going to be?'

'You should've been on the ten o'clock boat.'

He blows across the neck of his bottle, sounding a note like a ferry blast.

'You're not funny!'

He puts the bottle on the rail and his face changes, becomes old. 'I got as far as the dock,' he says, 'and came back. I've got nowhere else to go.'

Neil comes down the ladder and across the deck, mopping his chest with a wadded shirt. He walks up to Sal. 'Give me a hand?' he asks. 'Lots of work to do up there.'

'I'm afraid of heights,' Sal says.

'The deck needs fixing too.' Neil kicks a board with the heel of his boot. 'Almost rotted through here. I ordered some boards, they're coming on the next boat. You can do the deck repairs.'

Sal turns to me. 'So who said the kid gets to be foreman?'

'The window frames,' Neil goes on, 'those broken panes . . . all that.'

I take my cue from Neil. 'If you want to stay,' I tell Sal, 'you'd better make yourself useful.'

Margot rushes up to me. 'I can work in the front yard –

clean it up and plant flowers. Make it real homey-like.'

'Geraniums would be nice, like there used to be. I'll give you a hand.'

So begins a string of days sharp with the smell of tar and lumber, dirt and sweat. Days of sawing, digging, hammering, sandwiches and cold beer. At night, hot and aching, we fall on the deck and listen to Neil play his recorder. I sit back to back with Margot, feeling the stickiness of her skin. The sky seems to open then, and a breeze comes down to soothe us like a mother's breath on a young girl's scraped knee.

Then one day the work is done, the house looks straighter, swept clean. Sal wants to paint the whole exterior but Neil says no, he's going camping at Gulls Point. 'The rest in time,' he explains.

'What time?' Sal says. 'When the moon is in the seventh house? I think we ought to paint now.'

Neil shrugs and goes inside. He comes out with his pack, tent, sleeping roll and recorder. 'See you in a few days,' he waves over his shoulder as he trails off. We watch till only his head shows above the dunes, then lose sight of that too.

Sal says, 'We could do it ourselves.'

Margot and I exchange looks. 'It wouldn't be the same without Neil,' she says.

'Neil, Neil,' Sal grumbles. 'What's so special about Neil?'

Into July. On the beach the volleyball nets are going up, and Margot finds a spot on a team. She's gone all day. I keep sewing. Just a few more things and I can take a load of stuff to the Cove. Sal has the radio on but isn't paying attention. He's drinking too much, I decide, and picture his liver swollen to a freakish size: the end of Sal.

I start taking walks to the dock to see the *Island Queen* arrive – once to meet the morning boat, another time the evening boat, then every morning and evening. In the morning the bay is clear and has an ordinary blueness that is comforting. As if the pier, the boats and sky have always been exactly so, will always be, and the ferry sliding in and out will always travel to and fro: an unchanging vista.

And yet the evening attracts me too, its softening light and last sparks; the zigzagging of small boats as they race for shore. The *Island Queen*, lights bobbing, slams against the pilings in the thickening dark. The passengers are nervous: Will the ferry land safely or not? Who will come to meet them? All so unpredictable as evening reels into blackness.

At one end of the dock is a bench, the same one from my childhood, and that's where I wait most days. Islanders go by pulling empty wagons, on their way to greet the ferry, and pass me again later on, their wagons filled with luggage and a knot of friends at their elbows. 'The city's a furnace!' the newcomers say. 'You're so lucky to be here.' They travel in packs and suggest to me a hulking spotted animal with flitting parts.

But one evening during the week a woman leaves the boat alone and stops at the foot of the gangway. Jostled by other passengers she veers through the crowd with her head ducked, as if she were passing a line of armed guards. She stops again at the end of the wharf. From where I sit her face is indiscernible, but I'm intrigued by her color scheme: orange blouse and a green skirt to her ankles. When the dock empties she notices me, lifts her twin suitcases and starts in my direction. She drops her bags and peers at me, her eyes wide and circled in black. I smell musk. 'Anna?' she says. 'Is that you? Of course it's you – what luck! I never would've found the cottage on my own.'

Helene. Here in Onlyville. *Why is she in Onlyville?*

'I'm so glad to be here, you don't know how glad. You couldn't guess.'

I blink stupidly, trying to form a question. 'I don't, I can't . . . but where – why?'

'It's so good to see you again.'

'But where's Dad?'

'Probably still in his office.' She hikes her skirt up over her knees. 'Look at this.' Her legs are covered with black hairs. 'It drove him up a wall,' she says. 'He could forgive me anything, but not hair.'

'You left him,' I say, a dream-image coming to mind: Dad on the beach in Onlyville, his severed heart in a briefcase.

'For good!' Then she lowers her voice: 'Wait'll you see my armpits.'

'But why?'

She hands me a suitcase, pulls me up and hooks my arm. 'We'll talk later. Right now I want to see the cottage.'

On The Boulevard Helene says, 'The houses are so cute, like out of a fairy-tale. Like any minute we'll bump into Goldilocks and the Three Bears.' The young clerk in Army clothes is leaning against the Mini-Mart. He stares at us as we go by, and I feel his eyes on the back of my neck like two sudden punctures.

'So I finally get to meet Sal,' Helene says. 'Imagine you in love with someone all this time and I've never even met him.'

We turn onto Atlantic Walk and turn again. When we reach the deck she spreads her arms as if to hug the whole house. 'I love it,' she says. 'It's perfect!' Then she runs to the screen door, leaving me to deal with her bags.

By the time I haul her luggage in, she's already sitting on the sofa opposite Sal, who has a beer in his hand and his heels up. At his feet the radio plays, medium low. She reaches forward and flicks it off. 'Now I can hear myself think,' she says.

Helene sees me by the door. 'Be a dear and boil some water. I brought some lovely camomile flowers – they're in the bag with the brown straps.' To Sal, 'They make a wonderful tea, very relaxing.'

There are strange things in Helene's bag – bottles of vitamins, Tarot cards and a book called *Open Marriage*. At last I find the camomile and make tea. I hear Margot coming in and put an extra mug on the tray.

Margot stands by the coffee table, fingering the hem of her shorts. 'At last we meet,' Helene says.

Margot snaps her eyes up. 'Dad told me about you.'

'Now you can make up your own mind.'

I serve tea. 'Close your eyes,' Helene instructs, 'and let the flowers do their work. Imagine a spot between your eyes, a yellow sun. Concentrate on the warm sun ...'

When I shut my eyes I see the house and each of its rooms whitely lit. I see the bedrooms, two upstairs and one beside the front door. I see the beds, one double and three singles, rumpled covers, flattened pillows, *every bed in the house full*. I concentrate: yellow sun. But what I see between my eyes is a series of metallic balls, each one exploding in turn.

PART TWO

FIVE: 1951

MY FATHER HUNG a framed map on the cottage wall in which the island is boldly featured, broad and round at one end, the rest straight and narrow. It looks like a question mark.

The thick part of the island, called the Handle, is thirteen miles across and ten miles wide. At its northern tip the Island Bridge connects it to the mainland. At its southern end is the lighthouse, a stone tower built before the turn of the century. The oldest and most populated island town is called the Cove, its prewar cottages in a deep recess facing the bay. On the map the Cove houses are dots bunched together on a curved part of the Handle. When I squint at them they form a sickle.

The Handle tapers into the Stick, a twenty-mile sandbar. At its tip is Gulls Point, nesting ground for sea birds. The farther reaches of the Stick sometimes flood during storms, so nothing stands beyond five miles west of where the Handle meets the Stick.

Our house is on the ocean, a mile along the sandbar, in Onlyville. From there you can walk to Newtown or several miles northeast to visit the Cove. The lighthouse is a long hike, but now and then we'd go there for picnics. We'd spread a blanket in the sand, surrounded by dunes and screaming gulls and touched by the tower's shadow. There would be sandwiches, ginger ale and watermelon, then a game of spitting seeds as far as you could.

On the map the Berman cottage is shown by a square, the lighthouse by a triangle. The ferry routes from the mainland to the villages are marked by three broken lines. The ferry travels year-round, except when the water ices up, irregular service during the week but more frequent on weekends.

Once there was a whaling station on the island; once pirates buried their booty in the sand. Shipwreckers and slave runners stopped here too. In isolated places there are still deer and red foxes, rabbits and snakes. Fishermen catch fluke and flounder in the bay, bass and bluefish in the surf despite the breakers and dangerous currents. The summer the map was hung on the wall, two islanders drowned in the waves.

❀

We left the cottage after lunch and headed for the crowded beach. Today Daddy was going to teach me how to swim. I walked next to him, holding his hand, while Mother and Jay straggled behind. My brother, who was four years older, didn't hold anyone's hand anymore. Instead he held binoculars and a long stick that he dragged across the boardwalk, pulling it over the slats, making a hollow clop-clop that sounded as sad as anything I'd ever heard.

Mother was in a bad mood. She and Daddy argued in their room that morning and hadn't talked to each other since. Now Mother walked stiffly, hugging a blanket under her breasts.

Suddenly my right heel was stinging and I tugged Daddy's arm, whining, 'Something happened to my foot!' I hopped to a bench and Mother hurried to sit beside me, stretching my leg across her lap. She bent down to look at my foot, and her hair touched and tickled my knee. She scratched my heel with a fingernail and I pulled away, but Mother grabbed my ankle. 'Splinter,' she said. 'Hold still.' She pinched the heel, drawing the skin into a bump, and I started to wail.

'Crybaby,' Jay said. He was standing on a bench behind me, playing with binoculars, pointing them at the sky and sea.

Daddy said, 'Give me her foot,' and Mother slid back on the bench. Daddy squatted in front of me. When he cupped my foot in his hand I stopped sniffling. He winked at me. I was going to be brave for him. Slowly he lifted my foot to his ear and shook it, frowning. 'Sounds serious.'

'Oh Daddy!' I looked at the hairs on his chest, short and curly pigs' tails, the way they jumped up at me when he breathed in.

'I'm going to pull it out with my teeth,' Daddy said.

'Everything's a game to you.' Mother walked to the edge of the boardwalk, resting her arms on a flat rail. Jay aimed his binoculars at Mother's face. 'Put that down!' she snapped at him.

Daddy kissed the spot where the splinter was stuck hot and

hurting under my skin. He squeezed the skin and my whole leg was trembling, his teeth nibbling at my heel. I closed my eyes and heard the breakers crashing in the distance. I cried out once and it was over. He spat the splinter into his palm and stood up. 'There!' he said. He showed it to Jay and then to Mother, who turned her head to stare at the sea.

Daddy helped me to my feet and led me around in a circle. At first I limped but then I was walking just fine, and Daddy smacked my bottom lightly. 'To the beach!'

Jay found a spot by the dunes and spread the blanket on the sand. Mother opened a magazine. Daddy scooped me into his arms and carried me over the hot sand, into the sea. Looking down from high in his arms I saw the sand grow dark and darker, foam around his ankles, then the water splashing up to his shins and whooshing away.

He waded in up to his knees, then up to his waist. Riding his hip I felt my legs in water too. The sea was much colder than I thought it would be, and I shivered once and braced myself. The water was rolling and powerful, it pushed me around in Daddy's arms and pushed him too as he danced back and forth, keeping his balance. 'Don't be afraid, I've got you.' A wave jumped up in front of us and he turned sideways, leaning into it. 'Hold your breath!' It crashed over us, plugging my ears and filling my throat, and I came up coughing.

He carried me beyond the breakers, to where the sea was smooth and green. He was standing up to his chest now. 'Come on, we'll practice floating.' He tipped me onto my back, onto his outstretched arms, my ears underwater and my body stiff. 'That's the way.' His voice was low and far away, but when I opened my eyes I saw him right there. The water lifted me up and set me gently back on Daddy's arms, again and again until, suddenly – no arms!

'There, you're doing it by yourself.'

I buckled in fear and my body sank. A net of water covered me, and when I tore at it wildly with my arms and legs, it only tightened around me. Daddy found me and cut me free. 'Swallowed a little water,' he laughed, 'that's all.'

He held me up as I lay face down now, my chin wet and my lips tasting salty. 'Kick your legs like a frog does, up-out-together, like I showed you.' And I tried to make my legs go froggy the way they did when I practiced on land, but how could I do it with water between them, keeping my legs wide apart?

'Together!' he said.

I tried hard and snapped my legs tightly shut, shooting forward like a fish and dropping onto Daddy's arms.

'That's good. Now stick out your arms, hands touching, fingers tight, and push the water away from you. Push it away!' Daddy squeezed my fingers shut, 'Like this, like this!' Like I practiced a hundred times before. 'Up, out, around, under, together, kick!'

Arms and legs going every which way, my body heavy, sinking again. I swallowed water, spat it out, and my face went under: water in my eyes and stinging deep in my nose. Daddy caught me again, shouting, 'Don't stop!' I straightened out but my body twisted, shivering in Daddy's arms, and I rolled onto my back without even meaning to. 'Okay,' he said, 'your lips are blue. Lesson's over.'

All the way back he was laughing and talking, telling me how well I'd done, how funny I looked when he pulled me out sputtering, how small and slippery I was in his arms. By the time I ran up to Mother and Jay on the blanket I was ready to tell them what fun it was, what a wonderful time I had trying to swim.

'We're back,' said Daddy. 'Miss us?'

Jay had an arm over his face and looked like he was sleeping. Mother kept reading her magazine, but her hand rose up to smooth my hair when I knelt down beside her. Gazing at the magazine I forgot about swimming. Mother turned the pages slowly, stopping at a picture of a lady in a bra and slip, and I wanted to ask how many years before I'd wear a bra like that, but said nothing. What if my question startled her, made her close the magazine and drop her fingers from my hair? The bra in the shiny picture was a pointy one, but some were round. I hoped I wouldn't have pointy breasts but round ones like Mother had. She was very beautiful, but Daddy fought with her anyway.

After a while Jay got up and walked to the shore, and I

followed him. 'Let's build a castle,' he said. 'You run back and get the shovels.' The castle we made was not very high but big around, with many towers, slots, doors and a snaky moat. I sat on the side where the sand was dry, building a wall around the moat. Jay lay down on his belly where the sand was hard and sloped to the sea. Water bubbled over his toes as he sailed a Popsicle stick in the moat.

Soon I was bored with the wall and leaned back, looking down the shoreline. I saw how a wave began to curl in the distance and kept turning, coming closer, growing bigger, until it was here and scaring me with its rumbling. I saw how figures down the beach were wavy lines wiggling nearer, getting fat. Then they were people in bathing suits, running fast. Then they were four big men shoving and shouting, tearing across the wet sand.

I didn't see them step on the castle and Jay's head, they were only a stripe going by. They left behind a ruined castle with flattened walls, as if a bomb had gone off in the courtyard. Water oozed into a footprint, big and deep, that covered the spot where Jay had floated his Popsicle stick.

He rolled over onto his back and I looked away. I didn't want to see his face. I heard his breathing, hard and quick, and then he pushed himself onto his elbows and coughed my name. When I turned to him he started to moan. He spat and wiped sand from his mouth and blood from his nose. I knew how it felt to have sand in your mouth – those gritty pebbles between your teeth and under your tongue – and started feeling sorry for him. I jumped up and told Mother that Jay's face was a mud pie.

Her eyes widened and filled with color. She ran to him and grabbed his arm, yanking him over the sand like a balloon on a string, past blankets and beach umbrellas, canvas chairs and picnic baskets, past ladies in ruffled suits and fat old men with white bellies. Daddy watched as Jay and Mother flew across the hot sand, then got up and followed their tracks. Time slowed for me as I trailed behind, making loopy patterns in the sand with my toes. I didn't much care what happened to Jay. He didn't seem to be hurt bad and all this sudden hurrying was probably for nothing. I wished I hadn't said anything after all.

When I reached the house Daddy was pacing. Mother and Jay were nowhere in sight. Then the patio door opened and Mother came out, her arm hugging Jay's waist, her lips in his hair. He was only ten but almost as tall as she was. Jay's face looked pink and clean, like someone had scrubbed it very hard. 'A few scratches,' Mother said, 'and a mouthful of sand.' She dropped her arm from Jay's waist and went to Daddy, leaning her head against his chest.

I smiled at her, hoping she would notice me too, but she only spoke to Daddy's chest. He answered her sharply, 'All this fuss!' and I thought he might have liked it better if he was the one with the bloody nose and Mother had been bandaging him.

She stepped back. 'Well,' she said, 'you could've been more helpful.'

'Just what did you expect me to do?' Daddy's voice was freezer-cold.

I backed into a corner. Jay crept away from them and sat beside me on the deck. 'They stay together because of us,' he whispered.

I didn't know what my brother meant; I didn't understand the strange behavior of my parents. Why did they argue and what about? And if it was true that we kept them together, could we also drive them apart?

Daddy walked over and snatched my hand. 'Let's go back to the blanket,' he said. One of my legs had fallen asleep, the other one was shaking, and he had to help me to my feet.

Jay drew his legs up and wrapped his arms around them; his shiny face fell to his knees. Folded over, he looked like an old rag doll. Mother came up behind him and kissed his head. She slipped her arms around his neck, watching Daddy steadily as we left the deck.

'Can we play in the waves again?' I asked.

'Just for a while, I'm worn out.'

We went directly to the shore. First I balanced on my toes, then my heels, pressing them into the wet sand. When the cold water rushed up I screamed and splashed, it was so much fun. I looked up into Daddy's face and he was looking down at me and laughing. I squeezed his hand as he led me into deeper water.

Now I was up to my knees in it, now up to my belly. Breakers fell in front of me and shook the sand. Water bubbled, speeding by to get to shore, then snapped back like a rubber band you pull tight and let go. Sand was melting under my feet; I was standing with my heels stuck in two holes. Daddy took my other hand – he was holding both my hands now – and we turned sideways, facing each other as in a dance.

'Hang on!' he cried as a wave caught me, slammed me under, splashed salt and sand in my eyes and roared in my ears. He pulled me into his arms and hugged me. 'That was a big one. Here comes another.' This one rolled smoothly by as I perched in his arms, my skin itchy with goose bumps. 'Back in the water,' Daddy said, 'you're shivering.'

I planted my feet in the sand and grabbed hold of his hands. I jumped when a wave leaped at me, and it carried me up and toward shore. It carried Daddy too, his fingers knotted with mine. We were flying now, twirling around in our water dance, our beautiful waltz. 'Again!' I said. 'Again, again!'

Each ride more wonderful than the one before. A little higher each time, scraping the sky, a little longer, floating light as driftwood. Then I would land dizzy and breathless in his arms, memorizing each sensation, the jumping up and lightness and the falling down, so that I would remember every bit of it forever.

I was standing again with my feet sinking into sand, clutching Daddy's arms, when a breaker rose, bigger and darker than any other, leaning back like it was drawing a deep breath. 'It'll roll right over us, don't be scared.' But my legs tightened anyway, and I slid closer to Daddy as the breaker reared and blocked the sun. I froze in its shadow, Daddy's fingers digging into my shoulders. When I turned to him his mouth was a thin straight line.

My body jerked as the wave dropped, and time slowed the way it had earlier when I wandered from the blanket to the cottage. Inch by inch, the wave opened its foamy mouth and then, with a growl, swallowed me. It snatched me out of Daddy's arms and spat me into the hard sand, licked me up and blew me forward. Then it sucked me back again as more water smashed down.

Such a heavy flat weight pressing my chest, a weight I couldn't push off. I knew there was air above me and I groped for it and couldn't find it, tumbling toward shore again. It was shallow here but I couldn't stand, I was too tired. I threw out my arm and no one grabbed it. *Where was Daddy?*

From somewhere near, Daddy's face rushed forward, wavy and blurred. Then it fell away again and I was alone.

A breaker dragged me into deeper water. I was calmer now, there was no pain. I opened my mouth and breathed water, opened my eyes and saw the ocean rolling gray-green and dusty overhead. It was quiet here. It wouldn't be so bad to stay. But Daddy's hand swam to me like a silvery fish and plucked me from the quiet sea.

It was worse on shore: people stood around me and the air was thin, my lungs hurt, my back hurt where Daddy was pushing down on it hard. The side of my face pressing the sand ached too, and suddenly I remembered Jay, the way he looked with his nose mashed, and wondered if he'd felt like this, so lonely.

When I finished coughing I sat up and saw that part of Daddy's face was twisted. 'Did I almost drown?' I asked, but he didn't answer.

The people walked away and I turned to stare at the surf, at bathers ducking under waves and moving with the ease of dolphins through the sea. Someone came rushing up to me then, Mother in a swimsuit and a bathing cap with the strap undone. 'I saw the crowd, your father, and I thought you –' She dropped to her knees and drew my wet head to her bosom, swaying like she might faint. 'But you're okay?'

I pressed my face into her breasts. 'I almost drowned,' I whispered.

She sat back. 'Tell me what happened.'

'We were playing around in the water . . .,' then my voice broke off. Mother was glaring over my head and her lips were tight.

'Don't look at me like that,' Daddy said.

'How could you let this happen!' Then she got up and ran to the shore, fastening the white strap of her bathing cap. I chased after her, waving my arms, trying to warn my mother away from the dangerous tide, but Daddy came up beside me and pulled down my arms.

'Leave her alone, she knows how to swim.'

I shook him off and stumbled to the water's edge as Mother dove into a breaker, rising beyond it unharmed. 'Come back!' I yelled.

She swam out farther, cutting through the ocean with powerful strokes, then her shoulders disappeared in the black waves. Then I only saw her head, white-capped, bright as a gull, floating slowly out to sea.

SIX: 1953

JAY SAID THE ISLAND WAS, had always been, a hangout for criminals. After the pirates and shipwreckers came bootleggers, smugglers and dope dealers. Maybe even now there were fugitives camping in Gulls Point and places on the Handle. His favorite game that summer was cops-and-robbers.

My brother was the bad guy, and soon enough I learned the disadvantages of being on the side of the law. For one thing, it was easier to hide than to find. Jay would duck behind shrubs, lie flat in beach grass, crouch under the boardwalk, lose himself in the crowd at the shore or dive in the surf, and I wouldn't know where to look first. I wore a sheriff's badge on my shirt and should have been bold and fearless, but mostly I was afraid I'd never find him again. Sometimes he would pop out of nowhere, leap through the air and tackle me, and his sudden appearance frightened me too. If he felt like it he'd pull my hair, twist my arm or even throw sand in my face – crooks were allowed to fight dirty but officers weren't. If I caught him I could only say, 'You're under arrest' and try to tie his wrists behind his back with a bit of rope. He'd always break away because he was stronger.

I'd cry when I couldn't find him, when I found but couldn't hold him, or when he pounced and hurt me. I cried because the game wasn't fun and I didn't want to play anymore. That made him madder than anything. 'Cops don't cry!' he screamed. 'They don't quit!' Then he'd shake me till I flopped like a beached fish.

Once he bit my ear so hard he drew blood, and I ran back to the house wailing, 'I'm going to tell on you!' I would've told Daddy if he'd been home. There was only Mother, sitting on a kitchen stool, holding a needle and cloth and staring out the window. She was wearing a thin white blouse, and through it you could see the dark outline of her bathing suit. It was late afternoon, the time she liked to go for a swim, but she looked much too tired to move.

'Jay bit me!'

Mother's head snapped around and her hair swung out in a wavy arc. She squinted like she wasn't really sure who I was. 'He bit you?'

'He hurt me.'

The needle and fabric dropped down. Her arm rose, the hand curving, and carefully I stepped into the circle of my mother's arm. I sat on her knee, my nose in her hair, and smelled the scent of Mother's scalp, the fragrance of her shampoo. It was earthy and sweet. 'Aren't you going to punish him?' I turned my head to show her my ear. 'I'm bleeding!'

She touched my ear and kissed the lobe, leaving her lips on the wound like she would draw all the pain away. The ear throbbed, I wiggled, and she pulled back. 'I'm sure he didn't mean it, he knows better than that. You shouldn't play so rough with him. Anyway, it's just a nick.' Her leg straightened suddenly and I slid to the floor. 'Stay away from him and you won't get hurt.'

I jumped to my feet and scowled. 'I should've told Daddy, not you. Daddy would've done something – Daddy would've punished him!'

'Daddy fixes everything,' Mother smiled, 'doesn't he?'

I didn't like the curl of her lips and how her eyes had frozen. I backed up to the patio doors. 'Someday you'll understand,' she called out, but I pretended I didn't hear.

Jay was in the empty lot across the way. He'd probably been spying through the window moments before. When he beckoned me I walked over, stopping several feet from where he leaned against a tree trunk. 'I've got something for you,' he said.

I covered my ear with a hand. 'I don't want it.'

He dangled something on a string, and it swung from side to side like the pendulum of the grandfather clock in the cottage. From where I stood it looked like a jewel, a blue-white diamond. I wanted it. I wanted something beautiful in the palm of my hand. Slowly I moved toward it the way you might walk in a dream, without feeling the ground shifting under your feet.

'What did Mother say?' he asked.

'Just to keep away from you.'

'Is she mad at me?'

The jewel swung from left to right, right to left. 'She's not mad.'

'Are you going to tell Dad?'

'No.'

'Promise me.'

'I promise I won't tell him.'

I was almost up to the diamond now and saw that it was really just a small shell. Jay opened the long string and dropped the necklace over my head. 'I made it for you.'

The shell was blue-white and pinkish, perfectly shaped without chips or scratches, almost see-through. Jay had tapped a hole in the top and threaded the string through there. The spot where the shell touched my skin, above the line of my bathing suit, felt hot and cold at the same time. I stroked the shell with a fingertip. Its smoothness was exciting.

Jay ran to the beach and I followed him. Over his shoulder he cried out, 'You can be the robber today!' and my feet flew. The shell bounced against my skin like the bobbing tip of a magic wand.

One morning we played in fog that clung to the island like a fallen cloud. Mother warned us to stay close, but we hiked to a favorite spot near the very center of the Handle. Jay called that place the Desert even though it was green with shrubs and small trees. The Cove was somewhere north of there, the lighthouse south, but we ran in the mist without direction. We weren't playing games that day, we were hunting for real criminals, searching the dunes for stolen treasure, for tracks and smoldering campfires. If we found a band of crooks we wouldn't turn them in, just watch. Jay might ask to join them, he could be a scout.

When we saw the silhouette of something peaked in the fog we split up, Jay approaching from the left and me from the other side. It was his idea to do that, and once he was out of sight I wanted to turn back. If I knew which way to go I would have run home without him. 'Jay,' I called, 'where are you?' The ocean surrounded me. It spoke from the fog, from all sides, but Jay didn't answer. Maybe he'd gone on ahead. I moved forward until I saw that the shape was just a lean-to. There was no light, no telltale smoke. Jay could check it out if he liked but I was staying where I was, lying on a dune with my eyes peeking over the ledge.

The fog moved nearer. It wrapped my bare arms and legs, and the shell I wore around my neck quivered on its damp string. Fog covered my face so I could hardly breathe. I rubbed the necklace, 'Jay, find me, over here,' but he didn't show. The shell was frail, its magic unreliable.

I scrambled suddenly to my feet and ran over the dune toward the lean-to. It didn't matter who was inside – Jay or thieves or murderers – anything was better than to die in the fog.

The shed was empty. Its boards were gray and warped, there were holes in the walls, no doors, and the roof was crooked, hanging heavy as wet hair. I circled the shed three times, as if I thought I'd find someone hidden in the fallen planks. 'I'm going to tell on you,' I said. But maybe he was lost too. Maybe Jay was trying to find me even now. Another minute and he'd appear.

By late afternoon I gave up and started walking back to the house. The fog had thinned; noises were distinct and could be pinned down. As long as I kept the sea over my left shoulder I'd get home. I'd been walking a long time when I spied the haunted cottage on the edge of town, a rickety place Jay said had never been lived in except for ghosts. 'They're waiting for you,' he would say. 'They'll fly out and grab you.' I never went past there alone, so I stopped short and sat down. Beyond the house I saw them, Jay and Daddy, running toward me. Next to our father, Jay looked small and spindly.

Daddy reached me first and lifted me into his arms. His heart was beating wildly. 'You're safe,' he said. 'We found you.' I stared down at my brother, who was peering back with narrowed eyes, warning me but pleading too.

Daddy whispered in my ear – the left ear, the one that still bore the mark of Jay's teeth – 'Did he run away from you, Honeybear? Did he run away and leave you?'

'I didn't leave her!' Jay cried. 'I looked for her.'

Daddy put me down. 'You can tell me now, it's all right. Don't be afraid.'

I touched the shell around my neck, hanging dull and ordinary from its string. 'Yes he did. He left me there.' I looked up into Daddy's face. 'I thought I'd never see you again.'

I was already walking away when I heard the smack of Daddy's hand on my brother's face, a thrilling sound that made me shiver. Then I saw the pale streak that was Jay tearing across the beach.

He must've come home again very late, long after Daddy tucked me into bed and kissed me, long after I'd fallen asleep to the sound of my parents clinking teacups downstairs. This is what they did sometimes, they sat at the table after dark and drank tea. And sometimes I would sneak out of bed to watch from the stairs as they hunched at the table, clutching their cups, their heads nearly touching. What were they saying? What were the words that rose like steam and sealed them in a gathering cloud? What was the force that made their fingers shyly creep together? At least when they argued it was familiar, bold and recognizable as a splash of blood.

Deep in the night I woke to a creak and lay still, listening to the darkness. My heart was beating quickly, already alert to something close and horrible. It grabbed me by the ankle and it jerked hard. I clenched the sheets but nothing slowed me, nothing could resist the pull of the vacuum at the end of the bed.

It had always been there, always waiting, ready to pounce some ordinary night after I'd dropped my guard and gone to sleep, waiting to attack in a moment when I felt safe. I opened my mouth in a silent howl as fingers clamped my ankle and I slid, inch by inch, along the mattress.

There were sudden noises in the room, grunts and squeals. Some of them were coming from my own mouth. Jay dropped my foot and clambered out from under the bed and through the doorway. Another minute and Mother was there, picking strands of damp hair from my forehead. 'Bad dream?'

I buried my face in her nightgown.

The summer I was ten and Jay was fourteen he made friends
with a boy named Rupert, nearly two years older. Rupert was
tall, his hair black, his face shaded with thick stubble, but
mostly you noticed what he wore. He wasn't dressed in play
clothes, but polo shirts and trousers. Even more exciting, his
father owned a sailboat Rupert could use whenever he liked.
Rupert was teaching Jay to sail. I'd run along the shore as the
boat skimmed across the bay, a black flag in the glaring white
light of the sun. I wanted a ride but was much too in love with
Rupert to ask him.

When I grew tired of watching them I'd head back to the
cottage. With Daddy in the city all week there was just
Mother to talk to. Sometimes she was glad to see me standing
in the doorway, looking for something to do. 'There you are,'
she'd smile. 'Come sit with me. How about a game of
rummy?' Mother shuffled cards slowly, turning the deck on
its side and slipping some from the bottom to the top, like
folding beaten egg whites into batter. The cards were never
mixed well and often I was dealt a hand a lot like one already
played, but Mother never seemed to notice. She'd rearrange
her hand often, taking her time deciding what to throw out. 'I
don't know if I should go for tens or sevens,' she might say. 'If I
keep the tens, I know I'll pick a seven next.'

Other times she didn't seem to want me around. I'd turn up
suddenly to find her primping in front of a mirror, adjusting
the straps of her bathing suit, running her hands over her
breasts. At the sound of my step she'd wheel around – 'What
are you doing here?' I'd shrug and drop my eyes and she'd turn
back to the mirror. 'So how do I look? How old? Tell me the
truth.'

Mother was thirty-eight that year, and though I thought
she looked it I knew better than to say so. 'Twenty-nine.'

'That young?' She'd walk up close to the mirror and gaze
over her shoulder. She'd study the bulge and curve of her bottom, pinching the lobe of one cheek. 'You're flattering me. I'd
say . . . thirty-three.'

Turning from the mirror, she would grab my head and kiss
me. 'Let's go to the beach, okay?' Then she'd pull a loose dress

over her swimsuit and pin a floppy hat on her head. She'd grab a towel and magazine and I'd follow the click of her sandals across the floor, pausing by the patio doors to catch our quick reflection in the beaming glass.

Along the shore, Mother spread the towel and I sat down. She took off her dress and lay beside me, flipping through the magazine. She was looking at pictures of fall clothes and her hand shook. 'I'd love a tailored suit,' she said, 'blue or green. Wouldn't you love me in sea green?' Then she dropped the magazine and stood up. 'I'm going for a little walk and I want you to stay here, okay? I won't be long.'

'Why can't I come?'

'Because.'

She stepped among the sunbathers, beach umbrellas and canvas chairs, then turned west. It was late afternoon and already people were packing up and heading home. I lost sight of her in the crowd. I closed my eyes and lay back, pretending I was drifting on the bay in Rupert's sailboat, that Rupert was saying, *This is how you move the tiller*, fitting his hand over mine on the long, smooth, wooden bar.

I couldn't say what finally made me sit up and look around, but when I did the beach was nearly empty and two silhouettes, their shadows close, were gliding along the water's edge. At first they were just dark figures, then they were a man and woman, then I recognized Mother in her floppy hat. The man was slim and carried something square and flat under his arm. When they stopped almost in front of me I saw he was holding a folded easel. They spoke for only a moment, then he walked off. Mother tossed her hat on the sand and dove into the ocean. She swam far out and swam for a long time.

Water streamed from her thick hair when she stood over me on the towel. Strings of water ran over her collarbone and between her breasts. She was panting and her face was flushed. 'Who was that man?' I asked.

'An artist. I ran into him on the beach, he was painting a beautiful scene. He's very good.' She focused somewhere over my head as if she could see the artist's picture floating there. 'I've always loved art, you know. Not that I ever thought I could *do* it, only that I would've liked to study it.' She pinched the bridge of her nose between her fingers. 'My father was an inventor. He never made enough to pay for my education, so that was that. But you, Anna, you can go to college when you're older, you can study art. Wouldn't that be wonderful?'

She flopped down on the towel and grabbed her magazine. What college would Rupert be going to? I wondered. And what would he be studying? I rolled over onto my back and watched clouds cross the sky, already gray and purple with the first strokes of evening.

It rained the next day and the next. Playing Monopoly indoors, I felt snug and sleepy, like the cottage was a boat and I was rocking in the cockpit. Jay and Mother weren't paying attention and I won every game. When the rain let up toward evening, Jay ran off to Rupert's house and Mother put on a slicker and a shiny yellow rain hat. She said she was going out alone, she wanted to see the waves rough and white-capped. 'Don't go out,' I said, but she only screwed her face up, mocking my pout. I stood behind the glass doors, watching the shrinking figure of my mother moving toward the beach, and wished it would start raining again, very hard.

On Thursday it was sunny and I followed Jay to meet Rupert by the bay. When Rupert showed he was wearing white – white shirt, white shorts – and like the sun he was too bright to look at directly. I studied the crooked toes of my feet.

'We'll head for the Cove,' he told Jay. 'I know a couple of girls there.' They jumped off the boardwalk and ran to a dinghy pulled on shore. They pushed off, rowed out, and climbed into the sailboat. I waved as it slid away, but no one was looking back.

I watched until they were out of range, then wandered to the edge of town, where the walk ended. I stepped down. Here the ground was boggy and I slapped through it, swatting mosquitoes that stuck to my arms and legs. I ran until the sand was dry under my feet, till I saw dunes ahead and beyond them the open sea. From the top of a dune I could see up and down the shore, Onlyville to the left, Newtown to the right. I was no more than a mile from home, the air was calm, the sun beaming, yet I couldn't stay still. I felt itchy, mosquito-bitten, and sprang from the dune to the beach.

I might have galloped all the way back except for what I saw from the corner of my eye. It looked like a sign stuck in the grass, and I stopped to examine it. Not a sign but an easel and canvas, a painting of sand, sky and sea. And something else, something penciled off-center, a rear view of a woman in a blowing dress, standing shin-deep in foam, one hand holding her floppy hat on her head. That small figure more commanding than the sky or ocean. I looked for the artist but he wasn't around. On the ground beside the easel, an open box of paints and brushes, a palette freshly dabbed with colors: he must have left in a hurry, he'd be right back. I waited for him a long time, then gave up and went home.

Mother wasn't in the cottage. Maybe she was having tea with Mrs. Chaney next door or maybe she was out shopping, maybe not. I stomped through the rooms tracking sand. I ate an apple, a cheese sandwich, leaving seeds on the kitchen floor and crumbs on the counter – who cared! It was after four and Mother should've been here already, at the stove. Wherever else she happened to be was the wrong place.

When Mother came in she didn't notice me on the couch but kicked off her shoes and marched upstairs to the bathroom, leaving the door ajar. I crouched on the stairs and watched her as she brushed her hair fifty strokes, a hundred strokes, two hundred. Then she slipped her dress off and stepped out of her bathing suit. I almost never saw her naked, but every time I did was as surprising as the first time. The dark skin of her arms and legs was so unlike the rest of her kept hidden from the sun, her dimpled spine and pink bottom. Skin like a baby's, the kind you'd want to rub against. Suddenly she whirled around and looked at me on the stairway. 'There you are.'

I peeked at her breasts, the bronze nipples and rosy flesh. Not quite bronze and not quite rosy . . . subtler shades. I ran downstairs to a rush of tinkling – Mother's laugh or the splash of water in the shower.

Supper was late but I didn't care, I wasn't hungry. I picked at my food while Jay had seconds and then thirds, his breath smelling faintly of wine. Between bites he told Mother about his sailing trip to the Cove, how he jibbed and dropped anchor. He didn't say what happened when they got there, whether or not he met Rupert's girlfriends. Maybe they just turned around and sailed back.

Mother was excited as she listened to Jay, her eyes as shiny as wet stones. She didn't seem to be hungry either and barely ate. Suddenly she sprang up, tugging Jay behind her, put a stack of records on and danced with him in the living room. I watched as Mother whooped and huffed and her skirt spread out and rounded like a parasol.

In the morning they were still happy. Mother sang in the bathroom as she fixed her floppy hat on her head, and Jay asked me to go sailing. 'We're heading back to the Cove,' he said. 'You can come but you have to wait in the boat.' Later Rupert only shrugged when Jay said I was coming along. He was wearing white clothes again and was carrying something under his arm in a paper bag. He skipped through the marsh and Jay ran after, motioning me to follow. I sat stiffly in the dinghy, then just as still on the sailboat, hunched down at the end of a bench. Jay was the last to come aboard. He raised the sails, dropped the mooring and sat down next to me. He made a fist and showed the ridge of muscle on his upper arm. 'What do you think of that, huh?'

The bay was smooth, the breeze good, and we sped off. 'Coming about!' Rupert called, and I ducked as the boom swept overhead and we changed course. When the boat heeled I mimicked Jay and sat on the gunwale, leaning back, my hair whipped like the tail of a kite.

The boat came around a point and slipped quietly into the Cove. Rupert raised the centerboard and sailed into a weedy spot far from the wharf and out of sight. 'You stay here and wait,' said Jay.

'Where are you going?'

'Nowhere.'

Already Rupert was out of the boat and wading to shore. Jay grabbed the paper bag and leaped over the side too. But he paused, looking back at me. 'Maybe you can steer later.' His face was white, his freckles black as he turned and slogged through the tall reeds.

It was past noon when I saw them again. They were empty-handed and rumpled, like they'd just been woken up. Rupert tumbled into the boat and weighed anchor; Jay hopped in and raised the sail. When I moved over to take the tiller he slapped my hand and shoved me aside. 'You said you'd let me steer,' I complained.

'I'm steering,' Jay said. His breath was sour and he looked mad. I slid away from him on the bench.

Rupert was sprawled across from me, his arms spread on the gunwale, smiling stupidly. 'Your brother's in a rotten mood. Things didn't go well.'

'Shut up!' said Jay. Then he was silent, tacking the boat across the bay.

Rupert's eyes were half closed and he was laughing to himself. I could already see Onlyville when he stood up suddenly, rocking the boat. In the bow he stepped onto the deck, feet apart. I heard his zipper opening, the sound of splashing water, then I saw the tip of his penis and the long golden arc of his pee. The sounds were faint at first and the scene remote, but all at once everything zoomed very close, became distinct: the dirt on Rupert's white shorts, the black hair on his arms and legs, the mushroom-end of his penis. He sat down again, shutting his eyes, not even bothering to close his fly. My stomach rose and I felt sick.

Back at the cottage Mother was dancing by herself in front of a mirror. The painting of the woman in the blowing dress, standing in foam, was hanging on the wall behind the phonograph.

※

Two years later the painting was gone and the wall marked with a rectangle where it had hung. She avoided that part of the room and no longer played the phonograph. This was the summer she put on weight. Her face was creased and puffy and her wedding band seemed permanently planted in the thick flesh of her finger.

Things had gotten worse between my parents: they argued every weekend now. The littlest things set them off. Once, as I sat upstairs and stared down at the old cedar in the yard,

Daddy came barreling outside waving a saw, his chest bare and his neck red. Mother loved that stunted tree – she loved it even more for its deformity – but Daddy wanted it cut down. From the window I watched a wild man I didn't know. And then another stranger, Mother, ran from the house and jumped at the tree, spreading herself between its trunk and the saw's teeth. I trembled in my seat and prayed that the man wouldn't kill his wife. He only flung his saw to the ground and stormed off as Mother shouted, 'Don't come back! Don't ever come back!'

It was the summer of the photo album, an album that I still have, when Mother spent long hours slumped over the open book, her mouth twisted horribly as if she had a toothache. Sometimes I would touch her arm and ask hopefully, 'Rummy?'

'Look at this,' she'd answer, not even looking up. A photograph of Mother and Daddy, young, bright-eyed, arm in arm, handsomely dressed in winter coats. A picture I still turn to when I want to remember them in their prime.

'And this one.' Mother at the beach, sitting on Daddy's lap; Daddy in swim trunks, bare-chested, waving at the camera. The glaze in Mother's eyes was something more than love – adoration for the man who'd plucked her from a sour girlhood and fashioned her into a beauty.

Imagine a nervous young woman, not yet twenty, with hair on her chin and upper lip like black straws. How her mother fretted and her father scowled as Sylvia plucked the wild hairs and they grew back coarser, darker, stiffer every time. When at last she walked into the tidy office of E. Berman, Certified Electrologist, she expected to be stared at and treated like a specimen, to be prodded, scorched, scarred and even photographed. But the man behind the desk stood up and took her hands. 'Please sit down,' he said, guiding her into a chair. 'Call me Ernie, everyone does.'

'He had the friendly manner of a country doctor,' Mother said one of the afternoons we gazed at the album. He killed the awful hairs on her face with his magical electrode. Hair by hair he redeemed her. Months later when he was through, when she was twenty-two and totally transformed, he married her.

'Did it hurt?' I asked.

'What do you mean?'

'You know, the electrolysis.' My eyes were wide and fixed on an impossible floating image of my mother in a goatee and moustache.

'Oh, he said it wouldn't, of course. He said I wouldn't feel a thing.' She paused to rub her smooth chin. 'But it did. Every time.'

And that was the first time, I think, that I thought of my father the friendly doctor as someone who could hurt you. A man who could inflict pain. I squeezed this stone of wisdom in a tight fist.

That was the summer I met Bonnie, whose parents rented a small house on Sailor's Walk. She was fourteen, a year and a half older than me, and had the heavy breasts and hips of a grown woman. Her favorite thing to do all day was lie on the beach in a pink bikini, and sometimes I would sit beside her wearing a sunsuit cinched at the waist and tied at the shoulders with string.

That summer Rupert bought a surfboard, and we often saw him riding the waves. He surfed when Bonnie was on the beach, watching him, then hung around her blanket. That's when Jay got to use the board. He wasn't much of a surfer, he was wobbly and couldn't stand for long. He tumbled like a stick in the waves, a bit of driftwood no one paid attention to.

Rupert was almost eighteen and handsomer than ever with a new thin moustache. Once, as I sat with Bonnie, he circled the blanket, sweeping us with his tall shadow, then fell on his elbows between us. He turned to Bonnie and said, 'Kiss me.'

I flinched, my knees pulled to my chest, tense with the thrill and horror of his moustache over Bonnie's lips. She slapped her hands on her mouth, giggling, and Rupert planted a kiss on the rounded crescent of her breast. Bonnie screamed and shoved him as he rolled back on his knees and laughed.

'Pig! You dirty disgusting pig!'

He looked at me, 'Now you,' and his hand shot out and snapped at the top of my sunsuit. A string tore and one side of my freckled chest was bared to the sun. 'A carpenter's dream,' Rupert said, 'flat as a board.' Then he turned to Bonnie again and kissed her squarely on the mouth.

I flipped my suit back up and ran to the cottage, eyes tearing, hoping Mother wasn't home. But she was sitting in the kitchen, wearing the shapeless muumuu she had sewn herself. 'What'd you do to your suit?' she asked.

'I tore it.' Avoiding her eyes.

'Don't ask me to fix it, I've got enough to do.' Then she flicked her hand, 'Leave it on the bed,' and I flew upstairs.

She'd said I was too old to share a room with my brother anymore, so most nights I slept with her on Daddy's half of the double bed. When he came home on weekends I moved downstairs. I stored my things in three different rooms, not one of which was really mine. The clothes I kept in the front room were old and didn't fit well, but those were the ones I went through now until I found what I wanted, a faded skirt and pink blouse, snug across the chest and too short in the sleeves. When I looked at myself in the mirror I saw a Honeybear of seven or eight, not an ugly twelve-year-old.

Mother was still in the kitchen when I came down. I should've gone right outside, but something made me stop short. 'They were laughing at me,' I told her. 'Rupert called me flat-chested.'

'Buy yourself a padded bra.'

'Everyone would know if I did – you don't grow boobs overnight!'

She turned her gold wedding band around and around her finger. 'You don't wear the right clothes, no wonder they make fun of you. Look what you've got on now – ridiculous.' I could feel my face hardening. Mother said, 'Don't pout!' grabbed hold of my right hand and slapped it down on the table. But when she turned it palm up, her touch was soft.

'Look,' she said, 'your heart line runs from here to there, the longest one I've ever seen. That means you'll have lots of boyfriends, lots of love. Nothing for you to worry about.' Mother opened her own hand and set it down next to mine. 'Look at my heart line, how short it is.' Then she drew a long breath and glanced at the clock. 'It's almost four. I'm having

tea with Mrs. Chaney next door, she's going to tell my for-
tune.'

She walked out. I sat at the table a long time, waiting for
her to come back. At last I heard a dull noise and Mother was
in the doorway. She shuffled in and collapsed on the couch.
'Doesn't look good,' she said.

'What doesn't?'

'The future.'

✿

One Friday night in August I walked on the beach with Daddy.
The moon was at its fullest point and beamed a white stripe
on the sand, a shimmering path. Daddy was singing, 'Blue
Moon,' his voice as bright as moonlight. But then it changed.
'You'll always be my Honeybear,' he pleaded, 'won't you?
Always?' and groped for my hands. I tucked them under my
armpits and ran away.

I ran toward the lifeguard's chair at the edge of town, wanting to stand high up and feel the breeze, hear the surf. But
when I reached the chair it was already taken. I inched closer,
recognizing Rupert and Jay, and crouched down as the moon
went behind a cloud. They were passing a bottle back and
forth and Rupert was laughing, his voice loud, 'Then I put it in
her mouth . . . !' After a while he stood up and peed over the
side of the chair. The moon appeared between clouds and he
looked fierce in the sudden light.

I watched from behind the chair as they scrambled down
and splashed in the surf and Rupert flung the bottle over the
crest of a wave. They were running back to the chair when he
dove at Jay, tackling him, and they rolled together like tumble-
weed until they were almost at my side. Rupert was breathing
noisily, trying to stand, but Jay kept pulling him back down.
Then everything stopped – the movement of the boys in the
sand, Rupert's breath, my breath, the boom of the surf. Everything still and waiting. A moment – only a second or two –
then the release that came with the bang of Rupert's voice.
'You're drunk!' he roared.

Rupert struggled to his feet and tore off along the beach. Jay
sat up, dabbing his cheeks like a kitten with the back of his

hand. I backed up into the shadows: he wouldn't want me seeing him like that.

All the lights were on in the house when I got there. It was blinding. Dad was at the kitchen table staring into a teacup while Mother, in her muumuu, ran around dusting furniture. She didn't look up when I passed by, and neither did he.

※

The following summer Bonnie and Rupert were going steady and kept to themselves, so I took to visiting Jay in the General Store, where he worked part-time as a stock boy. He let me spray the vegetables, stack cans and stomp boxes. He even bought me ice cream cones, but usually we just swiped things – pencils, hair clips, chocolate bars. I thought of these as stolen treasure. They reminded me of cops-and-robbers and chasing him among the dunes, a time that already seemed like ancient history.

We could've taken anything. Mr. Wagner, who owned the store, sat at the checkout reading the paper and never looked up. You got the feeling he didn't dare, that if he looked too hard at things they'd shatter into pieces. Once I stole a paperback because I liked the illustration on the front: a blonde in a purple V-neck, her throat long and pale and her eyes closed, lips parted as in sleep; a black man leaning over her, his mouth on her neck. The book itself was disappointing. It had to do with racial prejudice in the South, a murder and a shabby trial, but by the time I was halfway through I'd come to only one love scene, much too brief. It might have picked up in the second half, but Daddy found the novel in the guest room and threw it out. 'I don't want you reading trash,' he told me. 'You'll get the wrong idea about things.'

That was at the end of the month, the last weekend in August. Daddy had come to help us pack. To my surprise he moved directly into the bedroom upstairs, and I was left to spend the night in the guest room. I wondered if Mother and Daddy were sleeping back to back, back to front, or if they were lying face to face, their knees and foreheads touching and their arms laced. I lay awake a long time picturing my parents on the double bed.

Sunday morning I found my father alone at the kitchen counter, drinking coffee. When he lifted his cup his hand shook. 'Morning!' he said. 'Sit over here,' his fingers dancing on a stool.

I sat on the very edge of it.

'Well,' he began, 'here it is, the end of summer. Guess you're looking forward to starting high school.'

I jiggled my feet on a bottom rung, wishing he would get to the point.

'So now you're a teenager, almost grown.' He shook his head my-my-my, then paused to examine my face, as if he were scouting for stray hairs. He was waiting for me to answer him, to reassure him, it seemed, that I was old enough to hear anything. I said nothing, turning to stare out the window. Everything was ordinary behind the glass, shrubs and grass, sand and surf, and long reaching arms of clouds.

His voice became grave – 'Your mother and I were talking' – like suddenly he was reading the Gettysburg Address. 'When two people don't love each other anymore, they don't want to live together. There's no point staying together once your feelings for each other dry up.'

That was the really horrible news, that love ended just like that. It dried up, like someone forgot to water it. You stopped loving and started hurting someone you'd cared about most of your life.

He asked me a question but his words were too far away to understand. I made a dash for the patio door and he cut me off, his hip hard against the latch. He grabbed my arms. 'I wasn't going to tell you yet.'

I looked out through the glass doors. The clouds were gone, the sky empty and colorless. My arms burned with a spreading pain. 'Let go,' I said.

SEVEN: 1958

MOTHER SAID the name one morning, apropos of nothing, as we dawdled over breakfast. 'Helene, that's it.' I should have been out the door by then, and she was already overdue at the Lady Luck Dress Shoppe. 'Your father's girlfriend's twenty-four and her name's Helene. She had a hairy abdomen but he fixed it.'

'Mother, I'll be late for school, and you're late for work again.'

'Some work! You should see the junk in there, all the seams unraveling and no style. How can I sell what I don't like?'

I stood up. 'See you tonight.'

On my way home I stopped at Lady Luck and peered through the plate glass. Mother was trailing a customer who flipped through hangers on a rack as if she were counting beads on an abacus. Mother glared at the customer's head, and it seemed that she would melt it with the heat of her look. In another part of the store someone stepped out of a dressing room and twirled around in a full-skirted flowery thing. Alicia, the owner, nodded and grinned and circled the woman with clumsy steps, a kind of waddle. As Mother's customer stamped out I heard Alicia cackle, 'This is your lucky day!'

Mother was fired within a month. Her parting words to Alicia were 'Goodbye and good luck, Lady Duck!'

❦

Jay held out a wad of twenties, but Mother wouldn't touch them. 'Save it for college,' she wagged a finger. 'Make something of yourself. You don't want to spend the rest of your life in a supermarket.' He didn't want to go to college, he wanted to be a travel agent and take trips around the world, but Mother didn't know that.

'Ask your father,' she whispered to me. 'What he gives us isn't enough, there's nothing left for nice things. Don't you want to buy nice things and look pretty? Everyone loves a pretty girl. Ask him for a little extra, don't tell him what it's for. Just to tide us over till I find a job.'

I met Dad in a restaurant and we sat side by side in a booth. He wore a suit with wide lapels and looked smart, like an ad man. No one would have guessed his job was plucking hair from women's bodies.

'So how are you? You like school?'

'It's okay.'

'Making lots of friends?'

I shrugged.

'Maybe you should smile more.' He stretched his lips to demonstrate, then he reached around my head and crumpled my hair in a ball. 'And maybe a new hair-do. Helene wears her hair like this, up in a bun.'

I jerked my head out of reach.

He snapped for the waiter and ordered. 'This is an expensive place,' he told me.

(In September, after he and Mother split, we had lunch in an Automat. Jay was there, he'd bought a dish of franks and beans with his own change. I had macaroni and cheese. Jay was silent the whole time, but I remembered to smile and ask a lot of harmless questions. Halfway through my stomach heaved and I ran to the bathroom. Back at the table Jay was gone and Dad standing, fists clenched. 'Your brother won't be joining us again,' he said.)

The waiter arrived with Pepsi and wine. I rolled my eyes, 'Too much ice.'

Dad had a large swallow of wine. 'Why are you in such a mood?'

I shook my glass and listened to the sharp click of ice cubes. Then I said in a careful voice, 'Mother lost her job.'

'Really? What does she intend to do?'

'Look for another one, I guess.'

He tipped his head and drank wine, his Adam's apple rolling like an eyeball under a closed lid. The waiter brought our food and my father ate in slow motion. He seemed tired through and through. 'So it's money you want,' he said at last, 'that's why you're here. As if I don't give you enough.'

I shook my head frantically. 'That's not why – that's not all . . .'

He stared into my eyes till they filled with tears, then put his arm around me. 'Honeybear,' he whispered, 'little Honey-bear. You're not like them, I can see that.' He stuck a green stick of paper into my hand, a rolled twenty-dollar bill. 'For you,' he said, 'not them. Buy yourself something pretty, make the boys turn their heads.'

On the street he hailed a cab, gave me money for the fare and ushered me in with a quick kiss that missed my cheek and landed to the side of my mouth. I leaned back on the lumpy seat and wiped my face. The rolling, lurching taxi made me think of the ferry to Onlyville, and though I was careering down a city street in November I listened for and heard the sea, I felt my brain go liquid in the hot sun.

I gave Mother the twenty dollars. 'Cheap sonuvabitch,' she said.

❀

There were other jobs, as a florist, as a cashier, a sewing machine operator. That one lasted seven weeks, the longest of all, before Mother refused to suffer another day of glaring lights and hammering noise in a factory. Her final scheme was to work at home. Jay had flyers printed up with our address and phone number and SYLVIA BERMAN, SEAMSTRESS – ALTERATIONS AND TAILORING in block letters. I passed out flyers after school and tacked them up on telephone poles. Then we waited. All spring.

Neighbors brought their mending, though surely they could have done it themselves. Then one afternoon I came home to find the living room littered with pins and strips of lace. A fat stranger, arms raised, stood in front of the floor-length mirror, draped in yards of taffeta, while Mother circled her, pinning, tucking and basting. A customer! But later, when the woman left, Mother wilted to the floor and sat there with her legs spread and her skirt hiked up to her thighs.

'How did it go?'

'She smelled bad,' Mother said, 'from under the arms.'

Mother's only customer, someone with stinking armpits.

It wasn't long before she stopped pretending she was waiting for clients. One day the photo album was on the kitchen table again and she buried her nose in it, breathing the air of nostalgia. There they were again, Mother and Daddy in winter coats or swimsuits, arm in arm or cheek to cheek, happy in an unchanging black-and-white season.

'We used to walk along the beach in the morning, collecting shells, and every evening, looking at stars. Spots of light, that's all they are. Why was it always so romantic, looking at the night sky?' She turned the page and pointed to a picture of me as an infant. 'Something I never told you . . . about the time we visited my parents after you were born, we wanted to show you off to them. Your grandpa was angry that day, he wouldn't speak to anyone, just sat in the living room frowning at us. Then at dinner he wouldn't eat and Mama started nagging from the other end of the table, "A whole day I slaved to make that soup, Nathan, eat your soup." When he started shouting I begged him to quiet down – "You'll wake the children, please!" – and he threw his bowl against the wall, just over Mama's head. The bowl broke, there was soup all over – on the table, on her – and she pulled at her dress, jumping and screaming "*Gottenyu!* I'm burning up!" I shrank in my chair and thought, *Ernie, stop this*, but it didn't stop. It just went on as usual with Mama crying, Poppa finally storming out, my heart in my throat. Ernie sat across from me, not saying anything. It was like he wasn't even there.'

Her face was closed, her eyes turned inward. I reached out and touched her arm, but her skin was cold and I drew back. 'That was the start of it,' Mother said. 'We were different together after that.'

🌸

In June there was a heat wave and Mother decided to take me to Onlyville, why not? We were already on the ferry when I felt suddenly sad and didn't want to go on. I sat on a step between decks and wrapped my arms around my legs. Mother put her hand on my knee and left it there until we docked. 'Someday the cottage will belong to you and Jay,' she said.

The house was dark when we got there, the furniture sprinkled with fine dust. I didn't want to open the shades and locked windows right away – I liked the sense of being in a grotto – but Mother ripped about in a frenzy, her arms like the blades of a fan. She sang as she swept and scrubbed, and I followed her from room to room, a toddler chasing a songbird, then hugged her from behind and kissed the base of her neck. 'Oh!' she said, wheeling around, and in the flash when our eyes met I knew she was seeing someone else. It was someone else she felt when she pressed her cheek to mine.

I wandered to the dock and watched for the *Island Queen*. The afternoon ferry came and went. Heading back I ran into Bonnie, a bag of groceries in her arms. 'I was looking for Jay,' she said shyly.

'He's working in the city now. He'll just be out on weekends.'

She shifted the tall paper bag. 'We only rented for a month, we won't be here in August. My dad got laid off a couple weeks ago.'

'My dad,' I started to say, then I caught myself and stopped.

We gazed off in opposite directions. Finally she said, 'I don't care much. There's more to do in the city.'

Next day I was back at the wharf, watching for Jay. I tramped back and forth on the boards, the old dance of waiting for the ferry on a Friday night. He was on the 7:10 boat – he must've left work early. 'Got you something!' he called out, opening his suitcase right there among the crowd. He pulled out a T-shirt, ONLYVILLE printed below the collar. Under that was an aerial view of the island, a drawing like the map our father nailed to the wall years ago. My eyes welled up and Jay clucked, he misunderstood. 'It's only a little thing, it didn't cost much.'

There was one for himself and a T-shirt for Mother too. They were all alike except for the sizes, small and medium, large for her. He unpacked them on the deck, where she sat with our neighbor Mrs. Chaney. 'Put them on,' he said, and we slipped them over our bathing suits. Jay took off his dress shirt and put on his, then pulled out a camera. He snapped a picture of Mother and me in our new shirts and I took one of him and her, but the shot I've always liked best is the one Mrs. Chaney took. Though we weren't centered in the frame, though her hands shook and finally the photo was blurred, she captured the three of us shoulder to shoulder, transformed by the magic of our matching shirts. Mother and I smiled at the lens and Jay grinned, giddy with generosity, his cheeks squeezed into golf balls. Picture of a happy family. Later I gave the photograph its own page in the album.

Of all seasons, summer 1959 is the vaguest. I remember how clean the cottage was – curtains washed, floors waxed – with red geraniums in the yard, but what did Mother look like at forty-two? Was her face lined, skin loose, her hair limp and white-veined, or did she glow with energy, a final stubborn blooming? And was she happy at all, even in brief spurts?

There were times when Jay delighted her with a wink or a joke, when her laughter jumped like a stone skipping across the bay. Once I saw her talking on the porch of Mrs. Chaney's house and her laughter happened suddenly, it shattered the air that seemed heavy and smooth as glass.

She slept alone those months, while I stayed in the room I once shared with Jay. Often when I couldn't sleep I'd find myself arrived in her room, not quite knowing how I'd gotten there. Usually she'd be asleep but sometimes she would thrash about, performing acts of grief with her hands – yank her hair, punch pillows – and once she even tore at her gown, like hers were the hands of a violent lover. Finally she sat upright and stared at me, unseeing, her face wrung out.

One weekend at the end of the season Jay showed up with a shopping bag, a suitcase and Bonnie. Mother and I were both surprised, we had no idea he'd been seeing her, but it made sense: those walks he took by himself in July, the evenings he was off to the Cove for a few beers. And all that next month, August, both of them in the city then, they could have been meeting every night. Mother's arm scarcely moved as she shook hands with her uninvited house guest, someone she'd met only casually the summer Bonnie and I were friends. 'Now I remember,' she said coolly, 'Rupert's girl.'

Jay blushed, averting his eyes. 'She's going out with me now.' He stood with his arms folded and his chest slightly concave, protecting his heart from possible blows.

Bonnie rubbed the small crucifix hanging around her neck, and Mother's eyes fixed on that. I could almost hear her thinking, And a *shiksa* too!

Bonnie did all the talking at dinner, while Mother only nodded in a tired way. For all her silly chitchat, Bonnie stuck to two topics, Onlyville and the weather, and before long she'd circled round and started repeating herself. 'But here at least you get a breeze, even on the hottest nights ...' Mother pushed her plate away and sat like she was posed for a photographer, grimly still, but Jay straightened in his seat and seemed reassured.

When Mother spoke again she said, 'Bonnie, your supper's getting cold,' and Bonnie paused long enough to fill her mouth with potatoes. Then she started babbling again. 'Jay took me to see *Gone with the Wind*,' she began, and at the mention of his name – or was it the idea of him alone with her in a dark theater? – Mother made a choking sound and shoved away from the table.

'I want to know who your friends are no matter what,' she told Jay. 'Don't go sneaking behind my back.' She stood up and marched to the stairs, pausing only long enough to ask, '*How could you?*'

Later I found Bonnie alone in the living room crying. Jay and Mother were nowhere in sight. 'Come on,' I said, 'it's okay.' I dragged her fat suitcase to the guest room and helped her unpack.

'I'm dizzy,' she said and crawled into bed, though it wasn't really dark yet. I went to fetch her a glass of water, and when I came back her eyes were closed. She slept like a baby, curled up, the middle and index fingers of her right hand jammed in her mouth.

That night I slept with Mother. We lay in bed back to back, but sometime before dawn she rolled over, turned me face up and put her head on my chest. I woke at once and didn't move. Her head was heavy on my ribs, her hair tickled my neck and chin. She was listening to my heart quicken, tapping the beats on my collarbone. 'Ba-boom, ba-boom, ba-boom,' she sang.

I sank my fingers in her hair, the strands crackling in my grip. I thought her hair would melt in my fist, that's how hot my palm was, how hard I squeezed. I thought that if she lifted her head, if she got up and walked away, my heart would break free of my ribs and follow her wherever she went.

It wasn't Jay's fault or mine, or even Dad's, but we blamed each other and ourselves nevertheless. If she came back to explain herself I don't think she'd be able to, she wouldn't know why she did what she did. An impulse? And suddenly she was under water, dropped through the ocean's skin and flowing through its green veins. Surely she changed her mind then, hating the taste of salt water, hating the thought of her bloated body washed ashore. Or else she remembered she was only forty-two, her life could change, unexpected things could happen, interesting things. But maybe all this came to her too late, water already in her lungs and her consciousness receding like a car speeding down a lane. And though her arms might've shot up, reaching for air as she kicked at the sea, she drowned before she surfaced. Her body never washed ashore.

This is what I remember: a Thursday in September, just a few days left before school. Jay was in the city, we were alone in the house. She'd had no supper, wasn't hungry, but said she wanted to go for a swim. 'You too,' she invited me, 'you can wade out.' Even the sky looked hot that evening, blue and red. The lifeguards were off-duty but the ocean was smooth, flattened by the day's heat. I didn't try to hold her back – nothing seemed dangerous and Mother was a strong swimmer.

I stood up to my hips in the surf and watched her swim far out, following the trail of her white bathing cap as she cleaved the waves. The cap was like a water lily floating on the black sea. I saw her dive and waited, calm, for her to swim to the surface. Waiting, I thought about nylon stockings, black pumps and cigarettes, boys with changing voices. I was fourteen, going on fifteen, and I played with scattered silly thoughts while my mother drowned.

PART THREE

EIGHT: 1974

'SUMMER COLDS are the worst,' Mother used to say. She would have gone on to scold me for spending too many chilly evenings at the pier, watching the *Island Queen* come in. 'That's how you caught your cold,' she would have summed up, and I would've admired her certainty, the way in which she overruled the world of germs in favor of a more personal wisdom. She'd feed me chicken soup and smear the red tracks under my nose with Vaseline. Then we would sit close around a hooded vaporizer, breathing the hot and blooming mentholated steam.

Now, with no one nursing me, I stay in bed for two days, dozy and bored, and when I can't resist anymore the sound of movement downstairs, switch to the living room couch. Sal walks by a few times before he sees me lying there propped on faded throw cushions, a child-sized blanket over my legs. 'What're you doing here?' he asks, lifting an arm as if to fend off airborne viruses, then he adds, 'Where's your friend?'

'Out shopping.'

'So, did you ask how long she's staying?'

'Not yet.'

'It's not like you invited her here.'

'I didn't invite you either.'

He bends over and squeezes my bare ankle under the blanket. 'It's just that we're never alone anymore.' He's barechested, in swim trunks, a towel hooked around his neck like a horse collar, his skin flushed. When he lets go of my ankle a cold draft circles my leg.

'Glad you're feeling better,' he says, inching toward the patio doors. 'I'm off for a swim.'

He's already opened the door when I wheeze, 'At least you could ask if I need anything before you go.'

He pauses. 'Sorry. What do you need?'

'Something to drink. Hot soup.'

He walks back to the kitchen. 'There's only instant.'

'That'll do.'

He brings me a mug of yellow soup with dehydrated vegetables, splintery noodles and pebbly peas floating like sewage on the broth. I take this as a sign of our relationship. Then he's gone. I stare at his retreating back through the glass doors, his shoulder blades and the cleft of his spine, until I lose sight of him and the doors fill with afternoon light, uncommonly sharp, a light that makes the room seem indefinite, like a blurred photo.

After a while Helene comes in, and I'm glad to see her. She's carrying a bag of groceries she hoists onto the kitchen counter and unpacks. 'Oh!' she says when she sees me in the living room, 'you're downstairs. You look better.'

'I feel lousy.'

'We're having tofu casserole for dinner, that'll fix you up.'

'I'm not much of a hostess either. You're doing all the work.'

'Since when am I a guest? And the way I just turned up like some abandoned baby at your door, I don't expect any privileges.'

'Besides, I'm sick.'

'Of course you are!' She sweeps across the room and sits on the edge of the couch, her skirt opening into blots of color, like a peacock's tail. Her large eyes, rimmed in black, seem extremely sorry. 'Summer colds are the worst,' she says, patting my blanket-covered knee. A knob of gratitude jumps in my throat.

'I think I have a fever too.'

She leans forward and touches her palm to my forehead. 'A little warm.' And though she's only eight years older, her motherliness is convincing. I might have crawled into her lap if she hadn't suddenly shot back and said, 'You must be bored stiff. Why don't I get my Tarot cards and give you a little reading?'

She vanishes into the guest room and reappears with a pack of cards and a thin book. Rearranging my legs on the couch she sits inches away from me, then shuffles the deck, counts out ten cards and lays them face up between us. As she bends low to study them I examine the gleaming crown of her head, the black polished hairs and the center part along her scalp as milky as the white of an eye. She wears a silver-threaded blouse under a loosely woven shawl, and her musky scent is strong enough to penetrate my stuffy nose.

'The King of Cups,' she announces, and I look down at a picture of a crowned figure on a throne holding a cup in one hand and a scepter in the other.

'Is that good?'

'He symbolizes different men, good or bad.' She opens the slim soft-covered book and reads aloud, '"The King also represents imagination, success and power, the power within each of us to do what we must in order to achieve our goals . . ."' Her voice becomes stronger as she reads. 'My God,' she says, grabbing my wrist, 'doesn't that give you so much hope?'

I stiffen at the stranglehold of her fingers, as if she would pull me out of my seat and into a world peopled by the Tarot creatures on the couch. And then I feel ashamed and try to relax my arm: she's still my father's girlfriend, someone I remember dressed in a blue sheath with tapered darts pointing to the astonishing fullness of her breasts. Someone I feel obliged to be familiar with. I make a joke: I say that when I think about men I don't feel very hopeful.

She draws her fingers back. 'I knew you'd understand. That's why I had to see you.'

'How long has it been, three years? Before I met Sal, for sure.'

'Too long.'

'We keep in touch,' I add quickly, 'don't we? Only a few weeks ago I phoned Dad, I spoke to him – to both of you – remember?'

'Your father . . .' Her voice drops. 'I didn't leave for a week or two, you ought to know, this isn't a trial separation – I'm never going back to him. I mean it.' She chews a thumbnail. 'Oh Annie, I'd like to stay the rest of the summer if that's okay. Just to get my head together, maybe figure out what I should do next.'

I start sneezing, once, twice, three times. Helene draws a balled-up tissue from her skirt and dabs my nose. 'Unless I'm in the way,' she says. 'I don't want to ruin your holiday with Sal, of course.'

'Holiday with Sal? I want him to go home.'

She looks puzzled, then, 'Oh, I'm sorry!' reaching out and hugging me as I squirm against her hot bosom. The breath goes out of me suddenly and I mold to the shape of her breasts. 'Is it over?' she asks quietly.

I mutter acknowledgment into her neck.

'What a shame. He seems so nice.'

'He *is* nice, it's just – I can't –'

Helene rubs a widening circle on my back. 'Maybe we can help each other.'

Yes, I nod. Oh yes!

When we break apart we're fidgety and stare at the crossing card again, the King of Cups. 'He reminds me of your father,' she says and I agree, a father-card. Fish and ocean, red ship, blue dolphin, blue moon; his baritone, his big hand, scratchy kiss. His girlfriend.

Going to live with his girlfriend. Going away.

'The Empress is your center card,' Helene says, pointing at a seated woman in a gown. 'She's a kind of heart card – follow your heart,' but she doesn't tell me more than that, she seems to have lost interest.

The Empress: rings and pearls and party dresses, taffeta, chiffon and lace, a crown of stars; slender neck and long legs, a blue heron, lonely bird.

Blue river, blue, he left her standing in blue water; floating, going under, gone. Blue lips.

('Your mother, may she rest in peace, used to say . . .' is how people remember her, by her maxims. 'Love is a woman's whole existence,' she would say.)

The patio door opens and Helene calls out, 'This one's Sal!' holding up a picture of a knight on horseback riding through the desert with his visor up, an orange plume in his helmet.

Sal pauses, peering over a beer bottle. 'Looks just like me. Where'd you get the mug shot?'

'It's Tarot.' She scoops up the cards and shuffles them. 'Want a reading?'

'I don't go for that mumbo-jumbo.' Sal shifts from leg to leg but doesn't leave.

'Come over here,' Helene says, 'we don't bite.' She speaks

to him in a mother-tone, although she's a few years younger. Crossing the room to an armchair, he casts an odor of hops and sweat.

Helene says, 'I don't really go for that mystical stuff myself, but I thought Anna would be amused. She looked so unhappy lying there.' She tips her head and fluffs her hair, which rises and settles like a wave. 'Isn't this cottage wonderful? And the island, such a beautiful place. You know, in all the years I lived with Anna's dad he never took me anywhere as nice as this. In fact we almost never went out, period. Work, work, work, that's all he knew, that's the kind of man he was.'

'Is,' I correct.

'*Was* to me.' She shifts her knees to face Sal. 'Dead meat.'

He shoots me a look I don't care to interpret. I start sneezing again, and they ignore me as I root through my pockets for a Kleenex.

'I left him yesterday morning – Anna tell you that? No going back either. When two people are bad together, drag each other down instead of lifting each other to new heights, there's no point staying together, don't you agree?'

I spread the Kleenex over my nose and mouth like a surgeon's mask and think of my father working late in his office that smells of lotion and alcohol, sweet and sharp. Will he sleep on a cot beside his desk and not in an empty bedroom? Will he try to get in touch with me?

When I look up again Sal is looking down at his beer. Helene says, 'So tell me about yourself, Sal. What do you do?'

'He's a journalist,' I offer. 'A very good one.'

Sal has a gulp of beer. Then he says, 'I'm taking a couple of months off to write a book.'

'What sort of book?'

'Something political. Also I'm thinking of doing a thriller, I've already started one.'

'Maybe a political thriller? Something with spies, that's an idea. John le Carré's a millionaire.' She opens a black folder on the coffee table. 'Is this it, the thriller book? Why don't you read us some of it.'

'Nah, I don't think so.' His eyes sweep across the walls, the windows filled with hard light. 'Anna's heard it anyway.'

'I haven't.' Helene hands him the folder. 'Read me some, I'm interested.'

'I don't know.'

'I'd like you to.'

He blows across his beer bottle, making a hollow sound. Then he puts it down and picks up the manuscript. 'She had the ripe blond looks of Cybill Shepherd,' he begins. When he gets to the bit about apple breasts and a pear-shaped ass, I honk my nose in the Kleenex.

Helene purses her lips, 'Go on,' but Sal shuts the folder. 'Well,' he sighs, 'we can't all be John le Carré.'

'Of course not,' Helene says, 'but think about this: each of us has the power within to do what we must to meet our goals.'

He drops the folder back on the table. 'Yeah, sure, but it helps to have someone believe in you.'

'Please,' I say.

Helene glances from him to me to him again, as if she's figuring sums in her head – one plus zero, one plus one, one plus two.

He stands up suddenly and I gaze at his bare chest, how smooth it looks; how cool it would feel to press my cheek against his chest. That would fix everything, wouldn't it, the sealing pressure of flesh on flesh.

'I'll start supper,' he says and heads for the kitchen.

Helene jumps in front of him. 'I'm cooking tonight,' she says. 'Tofu and brown rice casserole.'

I wait for Sal to roll his eyes and screw up his lips, but his face is still. 'Come join me,' she tells him, 'there's lots to do.' He follows her into the kitchen and I twist on the couch for a better view, but at such a distance, in smudged light, it's hard to discern small acts.

The rap of the knife on the cutting board, the hiss of running water and the opening and slamming of drawers remind me of family dinners long ago. Of sitting between Mother and Daddy, heads lowered over our plates as if in prayer.

'Here,' Helene is saying, handing Sal a knife, 'you can cut the onions, they make me cry.' I hear the click of it, chop-chop-chop, and see the pumping of Sal's arm, then she commands, 'Smaller – let me do it.' He mumbles in reply and she counters with a laugh like the ring of two glasses touching in a toast. To love! to health! the future! As Sal steps aside he brushes his hand across the back of her waist, and something crackles in the air. I hear it.

She tosses her head and takes the knife, the blade tapping the wooden board. The only sound. Suddenly she cries out. Then, in a thin voice, 'My thumb, it's bleeding.'

Sal grabbing her by the wrist, her hand in the sink, in a stream of water. Sal yanking open a drawer, squeezing her thumb, taping the wound and guiding her to a kitchen stool. 'There,' he says. He's breathing hard. Helene sits down gingerly, her finger raised like she's thumbing a ride, the round pink tip of the digit peeking over its bandage. She is shivering. I see it – feel it – the slight shimmy of her hair, the quick dance of her body, and I start shuddering too, jamming the blanket around my legs, but it doesn't help.

She slides off the stool, her skirt swishing against the wood with a liquid sound, holding her bandaged thumb in front of her like a torch. Her hair and shawl, her silvery blouse, flowing skirt: she crosses the room like someone walking in a dream, a Tarot queen, a creature risen from the sea.

She kneels beside the sofa, slips her arm around my back and draws me close. 'You're cold,' she says. Opening the shawl she hoods it over our heads. It radiates heat, as if there weren't round holes between its stitches but panes of glass catching the last of the sun's rays. In the silence I hear my heartbeat, I hear the surf, the murmur and crash of an old machine.

I sleep late the next morning and stay in bed long after I'm awake, Sal's pillow bunched in my arms. A scent of him on the pillowcase, faintly sour. From downstairs I hear the drumming of his voice. I hear Helene, her ringing laugh, and the drone of the radio. The pillow grows warm in my arms and under the blanket I start to sweat. I kick my legs and free myself from the sticky comfort of the bed. I dress in shorts and the ONLYVILLE T-shirt Jay bought me years ago, its letters partly missing now, looking like a jumbled spread of toothpicks. It pleases me to put it on, to recall the evening Mother, Jay and I posed for photographs in our matching shirts.

Helene sits at one end of the kitchen counter drawing curlicues in the air with a lit cigarette, her bandaged thumb chasing the coils, while Sal sits at the other end. She breaks off mid-sentence when I walk in and tells me, 'I'm smoking again. Do you believe it?' To Sal: 'I haven't touched a cigarette in years, but now, well ...'

'You're ending a relationship,' he says in a serious voice. 'That's always hard, a difficult time ...'

I pour myself a coffee. Helene nods vigorously as Sal goes on, '... not the time to worry about your vices. A painful business, breaking up. You think it's better to stay together than go through all that misery, but maybe it's not.'

'I've made my decision,' Helene says. She draws long and noisily on her cigarette.

'You're very brave,' Sal says.

She smiles at me. 'It's kind of Anna to let me stay. It makes it so much easier to have a place to go and to be with people who understand.'

I don't smile back at her. I grab my cup and hurry out to drink my coffee on the deck. To wash down the ball in my throat. To blink away the beauty of Helene's eyes.

Will he offer to cook brunch for her? *How do you like your eggs, Helene? Whole wheat toast and sliced tomatoes? Gooseberry jam?* And though my stomach's knotted up, it's rumbling too, remembering – crying out for – Sal's food.

She likes her toast buttered and her eggs fried, I could tell him. I was the one who made breakfast when I lived with Dad and Helene. She'd never eat the crusts of her bread and Dad wouldn't eat his egg whites, so he would pick the crusts from her plate and she would pick the whites from his. Sometimes they would lick each other's fingers clean like a pair of lovesick teenagers – enough to kill my appetite for the rest of the day.

I throw my coffee cup over the rail and it arcs against the sky, leaving a dark trail of falling drops. It slams into a mound of sand, then rolls out of sight. When I finally recover it and see that the handle is cracked, I sit down in the sand and cry.

Later I go to the phone booth, wanting more than anything to talk to Dad.

'Anna! Thank God!' he says. 'I was thinking how can I get in touch with you, who do I know on the island with a telephone. Anna, the most terrible thing – Helene's gone.'

My heart jumps. Should I say, She's here in Onlyville, come get her, tell her you love her, promise to spend more time with her and take her away? Remembering my dream-image, the man with his heart in a briefcase and the drip-drip-drip of blood . . . the best thing for everyone, a reconciliation.

But I don't mention Helene's name. I won't tell him what I know – I'll keep them apart. And my cheeks are suddenly hot with the thrill of my silence.

'. . . not a word, not even a note. How can a woman be so cruel?'

I cluck my tongue.

'So when are you coming home?'

'I can't leave yet. But when I do I want to stay with you a while, if that's okay. Till I get a job and find my own place.'

'Stay as long as you want to. You think I like living alone?'

'It takes getting used to, I guess.'

'You don't get used to being lonely, no one does. But now you're coming home I feel better already.'

And it seems to me it won't be long before he stops missing Helene. It seems that things will be the way they once were.

I leave the booth and walk to the shore, drawn to the shininess of the beach. Dark figures speckle the sand like a pattern on linoleum. At the foot of the dunes, the slim posts of a volleyball net. Coming near I see the tanned players in their too-tiny bathing suits, crouched and ready or already sprung. I see the tight knotted string, the ball wobbling over the net. Margot, in her striped bikini, legs flexed and arms pumping, doesn't notice me watching from the sidelines.

Her team wins fifteen-twelve to whoops and shouts of 'Rematch!' to back-slapping, bottom-slapping and someone chasing Margot, tripping her into the sand. She slides out from under him and he rolls over lazily, gazing unintentionally into my eyes, his face bronze and round as a penny.

'That's my aunt,' Margot says, giggling.

Someone calls them back to the court, another game is starting up. The young athlete skips to his feet, but Margot shakes her head, 'I'm beat.'

'Come on, we'll be short!'

She gives me a nudge, 'You go.'

'No way. I haven't played volleyball since high school.'

The other members of Margot's team are already in position, watching us. 'You're holding up the game,' she says.

'No, I couldn't,' my legs suddenly bowed. 'No, I'll miss the ball, they'll laugh at me.'

'Just until I catch my breath,' and she shoves me into a rear corner of the court. Immediately the ball is served and starts bobbing across the net – pop, pop, slam! – as I bend my knees and lean forward, imitating the others, as I lock my hands together with my forearms flat and parallel. My knees creak, my heart thrums, and I feel the sun on my back like a steel plate. With luck and a strong northerly wind, the ball will never reach me.

But then it does. 'Yours!' someone screeches and the ball thwacks against my arms, sending shock waves through my bones. It bounces off and into the sand, spinning like a child's top. 'Point!' someone calls out.

After that the ball keeps coming at me and my teammates have to work hard to stop me from handling it. Whatever my position is, two or three of them circle me. 'Mine!' they yell as I brace my arms. 'Got it!' bumping me aside. I glance at Margot pleadingly, motioning her to take my place, but she mouths back Not yet. Our team is losing badly.

I'd like to say that when it's my turn to serve I drive the ball hard and low over the net to score a point and redeem myself, but what I actually do is slam it into the net. The game is nearly over by then, no more humiliations likely. The other players crowd the net, jumping at it, spiking the ball in a series of maneuvers that I watch indifferently, as if I were back on the sidelines. How important is beach volleyball after all in the scheme of things? And if I'm going to be rejected, why not for a bad serve instead of for some greater personal defect?

While I ponder all this the ball whips across the net and over the heads of my teammates, speeding toward an unguarded patch of sand at the edge of the court. I see the frozen faces of the tangled players at the net and hear someone squeal 'Game!' as I dive for the ball with abandon, cleaving the sand like the prow of a ship, sending a gritty spray into my eyes and mouth. I don't expect to touch the ball and when it bangs against my wrists and rebounds over the net, I'm the last to know where it went, the last to understand what all the noise is about and why I'm hoisted out of the sand, hugged, whacked and applauded. Why Margot beams at me, 'Great save!' before resuming her place on the team to finish the game.

Soon I decide that although my save was an accident, the plunge I made was a daring and exuberant act! I fall back on my elbows, smiling, digging into the hot sand, and listen to the notes of satisfaction playing in my head.

Later Margot walks with me along the beach. She's silent at first, but then says, 'I was proud of you ... back there.'

'Thanks.'

'I didn't think you'd play.'

'I didn't exactly volunteer.'

'Still, there's lots who wouldn't have no matter what. I mean, can you imagine Helene with a volleyball? She'd worry about her nails and getting sand in her hair.'

'Even so ...'

'Yeah, I know what you're going to say – maybe she's a nice person anyway. That's the way Dad talks about his girlfriend Isadora, "Maybe she's a nice person even if you don't like the way she looks."'

'How does she look?' I can't help asking.

Margot cups her hands a foot in front of her chest. 'She comes out to here, like Helene does. Dad picks his girlfriends by their bra sizes. Also they have to be slutty when he starts going out with them – too much makeup, tight skirts – then he tells them how to dress and how to do their faces, he gives them that "natural beauty" shit. Natural beauty, natural food, that's his answer for everything.'

My mind wanders, switching to thoughts of Ernie and young Sylvia: Dad inviting her into his office, removing the hairs on Mother's chin, making her better than she was – a real beauty. What he did for Helene too, plucking hair from her abdomen. So they would be grateful and never leave him. So he would never be alone.

'Do you hate Helene?' Margot asks.

'I don't know . . . sometimes.'

'I hate Isadora almost always.'

I stop and take Margot's hand, wanting to say something wise and soothing, something grown-up, but say instead, 'Let's have lunch in the Sea Breeze.'

She peeks over my shoulder. 'Don't look now but guess who's in the water showing off her boobs.'

I turn around: Helene in profile, up to her knees in white foam, arms outstretched and her breasts rounded over the top of her bathing suit. A big straw hat on her head. What comes to mind is the painting that once hung by the phonograph, that picture of a woman standing shin-deep in the ocean in a blowing dress and floppy hat. What comes to mind is someone tucking you in at night, playing cards with you, cooking meals: those small acts of comfort.

The Sea Breeze has an L-shaped counter and glass bottles on glass shelves, their shapes repeated in a mirror behind the bar. We sit at a table overlooking the bay and order burgers deluxe, the waiter smiling, unseeing, California dreamin', as he backs away. How postcard-bright and beautiful the bay looks: polished boats and sails waving blue and white, yellow and green. A sign hanging outdoors rocks on its hinges, and a breeze rounds the window screens into puffed cheeks.

Margot says, 'Are you going to live here forever?' and I start because I was thinking, I could stay for ever and ever.

'Why do you want to know?'

'I thought . . . I was thinking I could stay here too, with you, I mean. I bet it wouldn't cost much. We'd work all summer, save up, and even in the winter if we had to – live and work on the mainland when the bay freezes over.'

'Live with me? In winter?' I look out at the bay again and two figures seem to flicker into sight, skating on the smooth water, sunlight catching the tips of their blades.

'So?' says Margot. 'What do you think?'

I straighten in my seat and shrug. 'It wouldn't work. The cottage isn't winterized, for one thing.'

'Neil can handle that. I bet he'd like to.'

'I didn't plan on staying here.'

'You didn't? What'd you plan on doing? Where would you go?'

'Back to the city, I guess. Stay with my dad at first.'

'We could live together wherever you go. Just like we used to.'

The idea hangs between us like a wind chime, something you could stir with your breath to make the most delightful sound or something blown into jangling.

'Well?'

'Your father . . .'

'He'd be glad to get rid of me.'

'All your friends . . .'

'There's only Neil and he'd visit me anywhere.'

'What about your mother?'

'Same goes for her. So that's everything – what do you say?'

'I'll think about it,' I tell her.

⁂

Helene and Sal are on the sofa, drinking coffee, when I walk in. Even though they're sitting apart, they're angled toward each other in a sympathy of shoulders and knees. 'Just in time for a cup,' she says.

'No thanks, I've had some already,' crossing to the rocker and easing into the damaged chair.

She leans forward and says, 'The most exciting thing, about Nixon, we just heard – the House passed an article of impeachment yesterday evening.'

'The House Judiciary,' Sal corrects her.

'That's what I meant, that House committee. Anyway, they charged him with obstructing justice trying to cover up Watergate – right, Sal?'

He nods curtly.

'They're voting tomorrow too,' she says. 'Abuse of power.'

'Impeachment's inevitable.'

She reaches over and touches his knee. 'He wants to write about it,' she says. '"Triumph of the Democratic System" – doesn't that grab you?'

I turn to Sal. 'Isn't that the title of the piece you started last year? The one I was helping you with in the city? The one you never finished?'

Helene looks from him to me. 'Maybe he'll finish it out here. This is a better environment.'

'You don't know Sal,' I say.

'Everyone needs encouragement.' She fixes her eyes on him again, her eyes flashing GO like a pair of green signals at an intersection.

He stands up, his chest high, but moves slowly to the kitchen and falls heavily into his chair. An old shoemaker hammering nails as he tap-taps the typewriter keys. As Helene watches with shining eyes.

I squirm in the rocker and its broken leg jerks out of place. I'm thrown against an arm and suddenly lopsided, dipped down. I think I'm going to slide off into a dizzying free fall – no one there to catch me now – my thoughts sliding away too: No, he'll never do it, *he will*; she won't change him, *yes she will*; they'll never be happy, *they will, they will.*

I keep away from the house as much as possible, exploring places Jay and I ran to when we were kids. August now, the season almost over, and I look at everything carefully: scrub and cedar, crowded streets, the clogged harbor of the Cove, the glass-and-pine cottages of Newtown. Knowing that I can't stay much longer.

Then something changes – the way daylight hits a shell, giving it the glow of flesh, or maybe a briny scent in the air – and I want to be part of this forever. I won't go.

One afternoon I cross the Handle and see Neil, a pack on his back, stepping out from behind a dune. I squint at him and his image wavers, floating up to me over the sand. 'Been camping on the beach,' he says, pointing east: the eastern shore, as remote as Gulls Point to the west.

'Is it nice there?'

'It's peaceful.'

'There's talk of a road along that shore to connect the bridge to the lighthouse, and something about a museum and visitor center.'

'Oh?' he says.

'I heard about it at the store. The islanders don't want it, of course.'

He shrugs off his pack and drops cross-legged into the sand. I sit down too, our knees inches apart. 'It wouldn't be the same place,' I tell him.

'Nothing stays the same. Everything changes.'

'That scares me most of all.'

He nods unhurriedly, and I lean over and touch his arms, his skin gritty with dried salt. The roughness and hardness of his arms reminding me of Sal's arms, of falling asleep in Sal's arms, of waking and twisting out of his hold. In Sal's arms: like falling and being pulled up at the same time. Sometimes I would think I was tearing apart at the waist.

But Neil's arms are simply there. Not exactly holding me, not exactly pushing me back. For just a moment I relax and notice his eyes in the clear light, colorless and sparkling, and his hair moving in the wind. Then suddenly I want more – to feel him really holding me – and I slide forward into his arms.

He pulls away and stands up. I'm blushing, thinking, God, he's just a boy, *he's Margot's boyfriend.* He looks past me when he says, 'Something must be bothering you.'

I make up my mind to keep the conversation safe. 'I've been thinking about the island – whether to stay or go.'

'Do what your heart tells you to do.'

'You're as bad as Helene – "follow your heart." What if I don't know my heart and can't decide?'

'Then you wait.'

'For how long?'

'Until you know.'

'You've been reading too many Castaneda books.'

He smiles at that, a sweet crease at the left corner of his mouth. Then he puts his pack on.

'You're going?'

'Yes.'

I don't look directly at him but watch his shadow sweep the sand as he wanders off. I holler, 'Are you going back to the house?'

'No.'

'Will I see you again?'

'Don't know.'

His shadow disappears over the ridge of a dune. I hear the notes of Neil's recorder rising and spreading under the sky.

Quiet nights. People speak of quiet nights in the country, quiet nights by the sea, and yet they aren't still at all but nervous with relentless sound. The hum of wind or surf, like the constant roll of machinery, while something else is screeching its name or pecking violently at the roof. Smaller animals skitter and bump, insects buzz and scratch the air, and I wake sweating, hearing the night. Next to me a rumbling creature takes shape, alarming at first, but now I'm fully awake and I know it's Sal.

How odd to find him in bed with me as if we were still intimate, as if my body still knew the curled shape of his in sleep. How strange and new the space running between us. I could almost turn and fit against him, but I don't. Quickly I get out of bed.

The hem of my nightgown brushes the steps as I make my way downstairs, sounding like a sleeve rubbed against my neck. In the kitchen I find the tin of Helene's camomile and make a small pot of tea. The sky breaks into light and dark, and I know again the familiar relief of approaching dawn.

From across the house a door creaks, and I think someone is coming out to join me. Moments later Helene walks by, unacknowledging: Helene in a white trailing gown, like an angel in a school play, her feet hidden under her skirt. I follow her as far as the door. She steps out onto the deck, facing the sea. A breeze lifts her hair and gown, one curling into the next like a wave stretching along the shore; the dark curves of her waist, hips and bottom visible through the cloth. A chill shakes me as I watch her, supernatural, fast asleep.

Mother, too, would stand in her nightgown near dawn,

watching the sky erupt into colors, wide awake and hugging herself or with her arms thrown up. Many times I'd find her there when I woke from a dream and looked for her or woke thirsty, needing a drink, or had to go to the bathroom. From behind the glass doors I would study every ripple of her hair, every toss of her head. Alone on the deck in the night wind she seemed impossibly beautiful, a woman of passion and secrets. How childish I felt in pajamas stamped with teddy bears, how thin my girl's body and how limp my hair. I'd cross my arms or raise them, just like her, but these were empty gestures to me, I couldn't enter the world of her emotion. I couldn't find that part of herself she hid from me, that kept her always, in some way, unknowable.

I never walked up to her, but I imagined doing so. Pictured myself tugging her skirt, pictured her whirling around to look down at me ... then my fantasy varied. One time her face would be fierce, another time preoccupied; sometimes even round and twinkling, tinged by the pinkness of the sky. From behind the glass I'd wish her close, could feel her breasts against my chest – or I would wish her locked out of the house forever, even dead. Then I would return to bed, trembling under the blanket, awake until the sun fingered through the blinds.

Somewhere in the cottage hinges squeak again, then Margot appears in a T-shirt and panties, rubbing her eyes. 'I'm thirsty,' she says.

'Want some tea? There's some in the pot.' I turn away from the deck, but the whiteness of Helene's gown is still in my eyes.

'Yech,' says Margot, 'camomile,' and puts her mug on the table. She walks up to the patio doors. 'Who's that out there?'

'Helene.'

'She looks like a ghost.'

'She's sleepwalking.'

'I don't see her moving.'

'That's how she got there, she walked in her sleep. She hasn't woken up yet.'

Helene turns with liquid grace and slips down the ramp to the boardwalk. Pivoting again she wanders out of sight. 'I've got to bring her back,' I say.

'Me too.'

'Not like that,' eyeing Margot's underpants.

She runs upstairs and comes down wearing jeans. 'Let's go.'

We catch up to her heading east and follow Helene to The Boulevard. The wind is in her gown and she seems taller and rounder. Margot says, 'What do we do now?'

'Well, I'm not sure.'

'Let's see where she goes, maybe some secret place on the Handle.'

But I grab hold of Helene's arms and steer her back toward the house. 'What'd you do that for?' Margot says.

'She belongs in bed.'

I turn her at Blueberry Walk, then up the deck ramp again, Margot right behind us. Just outside the screen door Helene stops and stares at me, her eyes wide, sooty with traces of makeup. Not a glint of awareness in her unblinking eyes, yet I feel she's peering into me, can read my thoughts. Knows all my suffering.

Margot plucks my shirt, 'Wake her up now, it's too weird. *Wake her up.*' But I don't move.

Margot steps in front of me and shoves me aside. 'Hey, get up, snap out of it, you hear me? Wake up!'

Helene's words, like bubbles breaking, 'Bup-bup, bup-bup . . .'

'Look at me, it's Margot. Come out of it!'

Her eyes roll up and her body sags. 'Catch her,' I say as she slumps into Margot's arms, Margot staggering under her weight. 'Help me,' Margot calls out.

Both of us propping Helene up, her eyes slowly focusing, then suddenly wet with consciousness. She looks down at us, shrinking from our fingers. 'What're you doing to me?' she asks. 'Don't hurt me.'

'No one's hurting you,' I say. 'We're holding you up, you almost fell.'

'What am I doing out here?'

'You were walking in your sleep. We're taking you back to bed.'

'Don't touch me,' pulling free and slapping her hands over her face. 'You want to hurt me, I know you do!'

And all at once her bones are somehow visible to me, her gown and flesh dissolved – Helene lit up like an X-ray. How thin her bones, how loosely strung together they seem: I could blow them apart. And I can't help it – I want to. I want to snap her into pieces, bone by bone.

But my voice is calm when I say, 'Go to bed now, it's all right.'

NINE: 1968

ALL THE NEWS was bad news, but at least it was happening somewhere else, on TV, where I couldn't feel the heat and rain of Vietnam or smell the blood. Besides I could adjust my dial, turning off the volume when the crack of automatic fire and boom of artillery became too loud.

On campus it was harder to turn the sound down. Sitting in the library, reading about medieval Rome, I'd be disturbed by students in the quadrangle – 'Hell no, we won't go!' 'Stop the bombing!' 'Black power!' From a window I'd watch them marching and wonder how I'd get through the year. One year to graduation . . . months of noise but then a job in a museum or gallery; the hush of art. But meanwhile in the quadrangle, 'What do we want? *Peace!* When do we want it? *Now!*' and I'd have to throw my books together and go home.

Home was where Dad lived in a lower-middle-income neighborhood forty minutes from downtown. He'd been there ten years in a rent-controlled apartment with a narrow hall-way, two bedrooms, a living room overlooking a courtyard littered with bricks and broken glass. Where he moved when he and Mother split up. Where I lived for three years after she died, until I finished high school and went off to university. Helene moved in the day I boarded the bus to New England: at last she had him all to herself. But I ruined it for her, stranded out in Regency Hills, Jay and Margot off to California. How could Dad have turned me away?

'Only a year,' I promised her. 'I won't stay any longer.'

'One academic year – that's what you mean? Nine months?'

'Our home is your home,' Dad broke in.

❀

Weeks after I moved in I came home one afternoon to find Helene reading *Joy: Expanding Human Awareness*. She said, 'Oh! Back already?'

'I just have life drawing today.'

She patted the couch. 'Why don't you come here a minute so we can talk.'

'About what?'

'About our living together, of course.'

I stopped where I stood.

'I see this as a special opportunity to know you better,' she began. 'A time for us to openly and honestly express our feelings for each other, explore those feelings, however painful, and so enrich our relationship.'

I walked away.

Helene followed me down the hall. 'For example, what are you thinking now, this very instant? Don't block it, don't be embarrassed. Tell me.'

I was standing by the window in the second bedroom – my old room, mine again – looking at the street below. 'You know what I'm thinking?' I said at last, turning to her. 'I'm thinking you don't want me here, that everything you just said is a load of crap.'

Helene cocked an ear as if awaiting further instructions. Finally she stepped up to me, lifted my arms and clutched my hands. 'Push me,' she said. 'Push me away.'

'What for?'

'Just do it.'

So I pushed and she pushed back; she didn't give me any ground. 'Harder,' she said. When I pushed harder, she did too. We met each other with equal force. I strained against her, arms tense, anger rising up in me and filling my hands. She staggered backward, grunting, and I pushed her like a bulldozer, steady and relentless, around the room. I pushed her into a wall, a door, a dresser and the side of the bed. She fell onto her back across the mattress, saying, 'That's enough. Stop now.'

I dropped my arms but couldn't stop the feeling. I could have leaped onto the bed and wrung her neck.

'Don't you feel better now? All that pent-up anger gone?' Her eyes, round with sudden fear, searched mine.

Lying on a blanket spread around her like a green sea, her pupils shrinking into points. How small she looked floating there, how helpless. Her voice tiny as she repeated, 'Don't you?' She was hugging herself and looked cold. I pulled the blanket over her, my anger giving way to something softer.

'Better,' I said.

🐚

Another time I came home to find her in a black leotard, sitting in the lotus pose on the living room rug. Her eyes were closed, her lips parted, a fringe of bangs on her forehead: she seemed lost in a sexy dream. When I dropped my notebooks on a chair she opened her eyes and smiled at me.

'Stoned?' I asked.

'I'm practicing Alone Time.'

'What's that?'

'You sit by yourself for thirty minutes and think about things, yourself and others, what's been happening in your life.'

'Don't you do that anyway?'

'Not like this – *seriously*.'

I was interested. 'So what were you just thinking about when I walked in?'

She glanced at her wrists, balanced on her jutting knees, then brought her hands together in her lap and said, 'Your father.'

Her answer annoyed me, so I scooped my notebooks from the chair and turned to go.

'He wants to do my bikini line.'

I paused again. 'He wants *what*?'

She ran a finger over her thighs and along the V of her crotch. 'You know, around here. So the hair won't show when I wear a bikini.'

'What if it does?'

'Your father says it embarrasses him, a man in his profession with a hairy girlfriend on his arm. Besides that he doesn't like the way it looks, there's too much hair, he says it's unaesthetic. You're lucky to have such light hair you hardly see it.'

I didn't feel lucky, I felt deprived. I wished the hair on my legs and in the hot creases of my groin was coarse and black.

'What I was thinking,' she went on, 'is I don't really want

electrolysis, I don't want him hurting me. I went through it once,' patting her stomach, 'that's enough for me. If it bothers him so much I'll shave.'

I edged toward my room. 'Got to study now.'

'I haven't told him yet,' she called after me. 'I'm afraid it'll make him angry. He really doesn't like it when –'

I kicked my bedroom door shut, then tried to read a chapter on Baroque art. As I stared at pictures on the page they jumbled into an image of Helene lying on a bench while Dad, in a painter's smock, gazed at her naked thighs. I slammed the stupid book closed.

Dad confided in me too, at first to say how hard my coming home was going to be on Helene because I represented his 'other life.' 'Still, better here than there – you had no business living out in Regency Hills. You never should've left school to follow that bum, that Henry, in the first place.' He patted me on the shoulder. 'But don't worry, I'll talk to Helene.'

At night I'd hear them whispering in the next room, their voices low and burbling, and sometimes I would hear their mattress bounce and creak. I envied them the things they exchanged in the dark.

Months later Dad confided in me again. 'Helene wanted me to do her bikini line, I said okay, business is slow, then she went and changed her mind. I think it's all that junk she reads – know-yourself, express-yourself – she doesn't know what she wants anymore. First it's *do it*, then *don't*.'

'What's the big deal?' I said. 'What's it matter whether she gets it done or not?'

We were sitting kitty-cornered in the kitchen and he leaned forward. 'Hair's important – hair *removal*. That's my business, what I do, I make a woman beautiful as she can be. Don't you think I want that for my girlfriend? Imagine the pleasure I'd get seeing her smooth and pink as a baby.'

I could not imagine that. I inched away, but he seized my hands and pulled me close. 'Take you, for example, those hairs between your eyebrows. They make you pinched and angry-looking – not very nice – but of course you're really not like that, you're a Honeybear.'

My hands felt swollen and hot.

'I could change that, remove the hair, thin your eyebrows while I'm at it, give them a more tapered line. You'd hardly recognize yourself.'

I slipped my hands out of his and turned away. Between my brows I felt the painful sprouting of hairs. I felt them growing stiff and straight as the straws of a broom. 'Yes,' I said, my breath exploding, 'take them out!'

So once a week I traveled by bus to Dad's two-room office where I'd been before with Mother and Jay or Margot, but never alone. The waiting room with its dime-store art and out-of-date magazines seemed unfamiliar, and I felt confused. Should I stand by the door? Sit in a chair? Go home? When Dad opened the office door and glanced at his watch, when he shoved his hands in the pockets of his ordinary white smock, I ran up to him headlong. He stepped aside and said, 'Come in.'

The blinds were drawn, the room bright with fluorescent bulbs. He gestured at the reclining chair and I stretched out on it gingerly. He wheeled up a stool and sat down, then swung the magnifying glass over my face. Twitching like an insect on a slide under a microscope, I stared back at him through the glass. His eye bulged, yellowish, with a black and empty center. 'Hold still,' he said, and my arms went rigid at my sides.

'It takes a true artist to do what I'm going to do to you.'

It hurt. Not just the first time, but every time. The needle coming at me, right between the eyes. That quick hot pinching shock, and Dad looming over me, his eye, his nose. I thought of him removing a splinter from my foot when I was young, how he'd kissed and nibbled my heel, then pulled the splinter out with his teeth. Hoping for a kiss now, for pats and jokes and tenderness – not this endless stabbing.

Every week I waited for the session to be over, for the moment when he shoved the glass aside and we were face to face, when he bent low to examine his work and I felt his breath. When he dabbed me with cream and my skin cooled, the smell of lotion sweet and ripe. When he nodded and smiled, his eyes shining. Only then did I forgive him all this.

He would hold a mirror up to me and say, 'Look. Already you can see the difference.'

I couldn't see the difference, just a pink and puffy patch between my eyebrows.

'Just wait.'

I took him at his word that he would not fail.

Helene and I never discussed my slow metamorphosis and I liked to think she didn't guess what was going on, or didn't mind. Sometimes she would steal a glance at the new curved lines of my brow. There was something knowing in her look, something shy and sulky at the same time.

Weeks passed. I was home studying for exams. The streets outside my window were mountainous with fallen snow, and a line of cars parked at the curb looked like toppled snowmen. In the next room Dad was lying in bed with a cold. Helene was preparing to go out.

'You crazy, going out in a storm?' he told her.

'One more day inside and I'll be crazy for sure.'

'So where are you going?'

'Downtown.'

'What for?'

'To see a movie, have coffee – anything.'

The hall closet creaked open and Dad shouted suddenly, 'What if I get worse while you're gone? What if I get a fever?'

'Annie'll look after you, *just like the good old days*,' the front door slamming on her last word.

I stood in my room and watched Helene cross the street and disappear, wanting to open the window and shout, *Come back, come back, I'm sorry!* though I didn't really know what I was sorry about. Then Dad called, 'Anna, please, a cup of tea.'

When I brought him tea he motioned me to the edge of his bed, 'Come sit down.' So I sat down. He lay beside me, propped on pillows. 'How's the studying going?'

'Fine.'

He spat phlegm in a handkerchief. 'I want to tell you something,' he said. 'You shouldn't take everything she says to heart.'

'She doesn't want me here.'

'She'll get used to it.'

'I don't want her to hate me.'

'How could she ever hate you?' He elbowed forward and

brushed a finger over one of my eyebrows. 'They *were* good old days, weren't they, just me and you. We always got along.'

He closed his eyes and fell back on the pillows, waving me away, and I tried to picture what he was seeing behind his lids. That high school girl with an armload of books, a motherless child who holed up in her room when Helene dropped by. Who cooked meals of beans and toast or scrambled eggs and canned soup. Who pushed the cart in the supermarket, bought vanilla fudge ice cream, folded sheets in the laundromat. And never complained.

The pleasure of sitting next to him in the front seat of the car or of holding his arm when we walked on the street, of trimming his hair when it grew too long or sharing a pot of tea with him in the evening. The way he spoke across the teacups, confidentially, would make my cheeks flush behind a cover of steam. 'The problem with Helene . . . ,' he'd say. 'That brother of yours . . .'

What he didn't know: how I woke to nightmares of Mother's body washed ashore, her eye sockets smooth as marble ashtrays. How I would catch her scowling in the oven glass or hear her bang her fists inside a washing machine, and be afraid. She didn't want me loving him.

I kept nothing of hers, not her white anklets, lace hankies, muumuus or floppy hat. An aunt came by to get her clothes, pulling beautiful things from Mother's closet – evening gowns, a tweed suit, a fur collar. I didn't want any of it, I didn't ever want to be reminded of her. But now I wish I had something of hers to hold – a music box, a silk glove, an earring.

I thought of her the afternoon Helene came back from downtown and sat with me at the kitchen table – how would Mother feel about me living with her rival? Helene said, 'What a storm! The wind is unbelievable. I could've held a sheet up and sailed home.' Her eyes were sparks, her breath hot; she warmed me. I was glad she was back. 'Mostly I walked around in it, the streets were almost empty. Imagine being downtown and no one bumping into you.'

'Helene?' Dad spoke from his bed. 'Don't you even say hello?'

She whispered, 'How's he been?' and I hesitated just a moment, then said, 'A pain in the ass.'

'Men are such babies,' she laughed, and I rolled my eyes in my best don't-I-know-it look.

'I bought you something. Wait here.'

She left the room and came back with a wrapped box. Inside was a purple scarf stamped with green lizard-shapes. I looped it around my neck and it felt cool and slippery against my skin.

'It's silk,' she said.

'It's beautiful.'

She pulled the scarf from my neck and tied it around my face. Then she sat back and considered me, her eyes traveling from my chin to my eyebrows. 'I love it on you,' she said at last. 'You look great.'

And I thought, Mother, forgive me, as I bobbed forward and kissed her cheek.

'Helene!' Dad called again. 'I know I've got a fever.'

'Coming, dear.' She winked at me as she walked out.

That night I woke to a dream of a quiet sea. When I opened my eyes I was thirsty. I threw on a robe and headed down the corridor. In the living room I saw a ghost and walked right up to it, setting a hand on its shoulder. The ghost was Helene. Wide-eyed, she turned completely around, not seeing me.

'Are you awake?'

She glided to a window and pressed her palms against the glass.

'It doesn't work,' I said. 'It's stuck.'

She left the window and aimed for the door, her fingers already on the knob when I stopped her, pulling her hand away. I heard her say 'outside,' the rest unintelligible, then she swung around and started walking again. I'd never met a sleep-walker before and didn't know what to do. I nudged her slowly to the couch and told her to sit. She sat down. I pushed her back, shook off my robe and bunched it loosely under her head. I went to my room for a blanket, half expecting her to be gone when I got back. She was still there, eyes shut, her breathing soft. She seemed to be under a spell, like Sleeping Beauty. Gently I tucked the blanket around her, as if she would break if I pressed hard. I dropped to my knees and lightly, quickly, gave her a hug.

❀

The man who taught me life drawing the spring of 1969 was a fortyish artist in patched jeans who liked to flirt with co-eds. Whenever he stopped beside my chair and guided my hand in sweeping lines, I'd picture him drawing *me* as I posed on a rug on his studio floor, naked under white voile. After he passed, the black lines on my paper would be wavy with blips.

The day I found myself in his loft it was not to pose but to look at his work, his paintings of body parts. Oversized arms, legs and backs – everything long and bony and pink – which made me think of cut-up chickens in plastic bags.

'I work from photos,' he explained. 'Project an image right onto the canvas.'

'They're so . . . unconventional.'

'Conventionality bores me.'

When I lay down it was not on a rug but on a Sealy Posturepedic on the floor. He studied my nakedness up close, and I felt the power of Art when he entered me and began to move. Behind my closed eyes I saw a fan of colors on a palette, saw my mother posing in her blowing dress and floppy hat. But suddenly he slipped out and rolled away. 'Wait a minute,' he said. 'Hold everything.'

He played with lights around the bed, then grabbed his camera and took a dozen shots of my neck. 'Beautiful,' he said. 'Your neck is absolutely gorgeous.'

His loft was close to campus and he said I could use it whenever I liked, the key was on the door frame. Often I'd go there to study and sketch, to get away from demonstrations and decrees, 'Burn your draft card!' 'March for peace!' 'Strike for ethnic studies programs!' Angry revolutionaries prodding me to *do something* every time I left a classroom, stopped for coffee, crossed a lawn. Like the black student in life drawing who followed me outside once, swinging his portfolio, and showed me a copy of *Soul on Ice*. 'Maybe you'd like to read this,' he said.

That book. Every group of students in the quadrangle

quoted from it, passed it around. Written by a criminal and Black Panther – why would I want to read *that*? I shook my head. 'No thanks.'

'Really it's not as bad as you think. Some of it's even hopeful. Stuff about the changes going on among white youth, an awakening of consciousness.'

I picked up speed, but the student kept pace with me. He dropped the book back in his case and pulled out a paperback. 'Here's a better one for you to start with.' He jammed it under my arm as I turned a corner quickly, then he ran off. I waved the book and cried, 'Take it back, I won't read it!' but he disappeared.

My heart was still banging when I got to my lover's loft. I sat in the center of the room and focused on the stillness. At five o'clock the heat went off, the room slowly darkened as the sun moved behind a tower, but I didn't turn the lights on. The pink body parts on the walls shivered and dimmed. From somewhere in the building the sound of footsteps going away, then everything was silent again, cool and dark. Soon my lover would arrive.

Most nights he was there by seven, never surprised to see me. We'd kiss, have a glass of wine, maybe take some photos, spend a few brisk minutes in bed. Then I'd have to go because he had to work. Make art. But that night I heard the key in the lock at six. He walked in and the room took on a purple glow, a smell of smoke and something sweet and swampy. A dark figure was at his side. When he turned on the lights I saw her clearly: younger than me and taller too, hair to her waist and eyes as round as doorknobs. 'This is Cheryl,' he said. 'She wants to pose for me.'

'I see,' I said.

'No you don't.' He left Cheryl by the door, hooked my arm and walked me across the loft. 'I need variety – understand? It inspires me. That's how I am.'

'You sleep with them, don't you. I can tell.'

He grabbed my shoulders. 'Don't be so possessive, so *conventional*,' his fingers digging into me.

'Let go,' I said, 'you're hurting me,' and he let go. Just like that. He let me run across the room, past Cheryl, out the door, and never said a word, never called me back. Just a word and I might've stopped, my knees might have locked in place, *but he never said a damn word.*

꧁

Dad and Helene were arguing when I got home. They were sitting side by side in two living room chairs, their fingers clawing the armrests, glaring at the TV.

'You're practically Neanderthal,' Helene said with a flip of her hair.

Dad's lips were trembling. 'You're turning into *that*,' he sputtered, 'that *shrew.*'

I hunched in front of the TV. A woman in wire-rim glasses said, 'Women must be dignified,' and I winced to think of the scene in the loft. 'The days of kowtowing to men are over,' she went on as my face grew warm.

Dad struck his knee with a fist. 'Bulldyke!'

Helene said, 'Why don't you just listen to her – she makes more sense than you do.'

Dad shook a finger at Helene's nose and puckered his lips.

'Don't threaten me!' she yelled.

I could hardly hear the woman on the screen anymore, her urgent message of hope and change. What was that about personal integrity, identity and self-worth? I turned the volume up high.

'Shut that off!' Dad threw a slipper at the TV.

'Leave it on!'

I stood and faced them, half risen in their seats, their faces pink. 'Listen to yourselves,' I said. 'Like children. Why can't anyone get along? Why does everyone have to be so damn mean!'

They dropped back into their seats. In the stunned moment I fled to my room, slammed the door and leaned against it, sliding down to a low crouch. Again they started bickering, and from the street the honking of horns, blare of sirens, rush of tires. The room too hot and close – like being under klieg lights. My skin was crawling, belly tight, my gorgeous neck was throbbing.

Bastard. You sonuvabitch!

I charged the walls of my room, kicking and slapping them. I strangled pillows, tore pictures, emptied drawers. I threw pencils, postcards, photos, underwear, a stuffed bear – mound upon mound upon the floor, like scoops of ice cream topped with glass. No one interrupted me. At last I fell, exhausted, and stretched out among the debris.

Later, when I couldn't sleep, I got out of bed and found the book that student gave me after class. 'I am an invisible man,' it began.

I nodded yes, feeling hot behind my eyes. Oh yes.

❦

We watched the evening news daily. Dad and Helene spoke to the set, they cursed and cheered at marchers and militants, never in agreement. Demonstrations, church services, candlelight vigils, Vietnam vets, students and senators filled the screen; smoke bombs and tear gas, helmeted cops and billy clubs – not to mention continuing coverage of the war: GIs and their M-16s pausing for lunch, running for cover, carrying their wounded buddies to helicopters in the field. Then the My Lai massacre was in the news, murder, rape and hundreds dead. We watched the screen, Helene cried, and even Dad had nothing to say.

He leaned over and took her hand, their hands becoming one mold, their foreheads touching. For just a moment she caught my eye – a dry, hard look – and the fear I was feeling for all that was happening *out there* landed heavily in my lap.

One night Helene said, 'We've got to talk, you and me.' She came into my room, swinging the door shut behind her.

'Sit down,' I said, clearing a spot on the mattress.

Instead she paced at the foot of my bed. 'This doesn't have much to do with us – you and me. We've been getting along fine, haven't we?'

My stomach flipped.

'It's mainly because of how your father's business has dropped off. He thinks he can do better in the suburbs. Not a place like Regency Hills,' she added quickly, 'something more upscale.'

'You want to move?'

She stopped at my dresser to finger a soldier doll missing a hand, and a small eyeless teddy bear. 'The city isn't safe anymore – marches, riots, bomb scares. Every time I'm out on the street I feel like someone's watching me through a gun sight. Don't you feel it too, like you just want to stay indoors away from all the crazies?' Now she sat beside me on the bed and grabbed hold of my hands. 'Don't you, Annie? *Don't you!*'

I drew my hands out of hers. 'Are you taking me? What about me?'

She picked fuzz from the blanket. 'It's taken longer than you said – more than a year – but now you're getting out of school and look at you, no job and no plans. Your father's worried about your future. We both are.'

'So I'm not going with you,' I said. 'That's been decided.'

She tore thread from the blanket. 'Now don't get upset. Think about it – what would you do in the suburbs? It's no place for a single girl.'

'Better I should live among the psychos.'

'You said you were going to get a degree and move on – remember? So okay, you've got your degree.'

I went to the window and looked out. Streetlights shone in the empty dark.

Helene said quietly, 'We'll help you any way we can,' coming up behind me. 'It's not like we're going to the moon, we'll only be a train ride away.'

I felt her hands, heavy and wide, sinking into my shoulders, and her bosom soft against my back. She turned me around and I let her. She drew me close and I didn't resist. She tied me in her arms and I let her do that too. She murmured, 'You can visit us whenever you like,' and I said yes.

'We'll be there if you need us.'

'Yes.'

'We care about you.'

'Yes.'

'We do.'

But I knew better.

TEN: 1974

NIXON ANNOUNCES his resignation Thursday night. We hear it on the radio, that sober voice, '...I shall resign the presidency effective at noon tomorrow.' I sit up straight: an electric feeling. The *President* is stepping down.

Helene runs to the radio. 'The poor man. He must be feeling so alone, so hated and humiliated. What if they bring charges against him, what if they lock him up – how could he bear it?'

'Don't worry, they'll pardon him.' Sal is on the sofa with his heels up, a beer bottle clenched in his thighs. 'And everything will go on as before.'

Helene turns to him, the radio in her arms. 'How can you say that? This is what you've been waiting for! Remember your essay, "Triumph of the Democratic System"? Now you can finish it.'

Sal slips the bottle from between his legs and empties it.

Margot says, 'Who's gonna run the country now? Who's gonna protect us?'

I cross the room to crouch by her chair. 'A powerful man – the President – lied to us, committed crimes, and we took his power away. I never thought it would happen but it did happen – right now! We stood up to him, we have power, people like us.'

'Don't believe it,' Sal says.

'*Yes* believe it,' says Helene, 'the people have spoken. No to burglary, wiretaps and cover-ups, no to abuse of power. The government has fallen and we're free at last!'

'"Free at last, free at last." You sound like Martin Luther King. What the hell are you free to *do*?' Sal asks.

Helene hugs the radio. She looks at Margot, looks at me. 'Free to decide.'

'Decide what?'

'About my life ... ,' her voice fading.

'What decisions can you make with Gerald Ford in the White House that you couldn't make with Nixon there? One administration's as bad as the next. You have no freedom,' he says to Helene, 'or real power,' said to me. 'You're kidding yourselves.'

'Never mind,' I tell him. 'Nixon's resignation means something to me. Really, I don't understand you. I thought you'd be elated.'

'It's over,' he says, 'the end of it. Endings make me miserable. I bet even Woodward and Bernstein feel let down.'

Helene sits in the rocking chair and buries the radio in her lap. 'I voted for him, for peace with honor, law-and-order. Now look at him, a lawbreaker leaving in shame. Who can you trust if you can't trust the President of the United States?'

Trust yourself, I'm thinking. You can trust yourself. All the mistakes you've ever made have taught you something, are leading you somewhere – trust that.

In the morning I turn up the radio and we hear Nixon's farewell speech to his cabinet and staff. He is rambling, angry, stricken, tender. He speaks of his father – motorman, rancher, grocer – and his mother – 'a saint' – as we listen to the quake in his voice, the strangled weeping. He talks about loss and disappointment, the need to go on. 'It is only a beginning always,' Nixon says.

Sal, Helene and I sit at the kitchen table, heads bowed. 'Imagine being inspired by Richard Nixon,' I say.

'It's so sad,' Helene sighs.

'It's not sad, it's not inspiring,' Sal says. 'It's embarrassing. He's a broken man.'

'His family will love him,' Helene says. 'His family will look after him, he won't be alone. I'd like to tell him to open his heart to Pat, Julie and Tricia, they can save him.'

'He'll always be alone,' I say. 'He's that kind of man.' Then I announce I'm going out to get the paper.

I decide to walk along the beach. The sand is hot, the same bleached shade as the sky, and I shield my eyes with a hand. In the distance I recognize Margot squatting next to someone dressed in green – the young clerk. Good, I think. I won't run into him in the store.

Back at the cottage I stretch out on the couch and open the paper. Yesterday's news: the text of Nixon's speech and a grim shot of him talking to the cameras. Sitting at the kitchen table Sal slumps in front of his typewriter, hands on his knees. Helene bends over him. 'How's it going?'

He reads aloud in a tired voice: 'He knew about the Watergate break-in soon enough and was willing to stop an FBI investigation of the crime, willing to thwart Congress and the judiciary, willing, too, to pressure the media into dropping the story. His was a reign of lawlessness and intimidation, of executive power unchecked. Finally it was that very press, that same judicial system and those members of Congress who brought him down. Now we ask, Was this administration atypical? Has the office of the presidency been besmirched or, rather, shown in all its meanness? Will future presidents be forever suspect in the eyes of the electorate? Or, by his shame and defeat, has Nixon strengthened the presidency, cleansed it and restored it to grandeur? Does Nixon's loss of power mean a triumph for democracy?'

Helene frowns. 'You haven't added much,' she says.

I fold my paper. 'All he has to do is answer the question now,' I tell her. 'Another line or two and he's done.'

'That's all he's had to do for days.'

He sinks lower in his chair. I get up and stand behind him, shoulder to shoulder with Helene. 'Maybe he could change the title,' Helene says, eyeing the page in the roller. 'You know, make it a question – "Triumph of the Democratic System?" Then he could end it right there.'

I shake my head as I read the final sentences. 'He needs to make a statement, give an opinion, an interpretation. That's what an essay's all about. Something like … the nation was in danger of coming under the total control of one man. Only the White House would be heard and any opposition would be silenced … Then he has to say how only a handful of facts and a few brave individuals changed all that.'

'Yes,' Helene agrees, nudging Sal's shoulder, 'that's it.'

'Just what I wrote.' He shoves the carriage to the right and rolls the paper higher up. 'It's all here.'

I read the page again. 'You need more,' I insist and turn to

Helene. 'How's this: The legislative branch deserves our confidence again and the press our admiration. The Constitution has been upheld, democracy has won the day, and we are free.'

Helene pulls her lower lip. 'Free to do what?'

'To love and trust, shape our lives, pursue happiness – all that. Nixon lost his power and we have found ours.'

'Beautiful,' Helene says. 'That's so beautiful.'

I give her a small sweet smile.

Sal yanks the page out and scans the final paragraph. 'Do you expect me to end with that drivel, that romantic pap? Don't you understand the way the world works? Nixon was sloppy, that's all, and two ambitious journalists got wind of his crimes and revealed them, catapulting themselves to fame in the process. You know what future presidents will learn from this? Not to uphold the law but to watch out when they break it – to cover their tracks. Not to loosen control but to tighten it. A triumph of democracy – ha!'

'You could write that,' Helene says as Sal rips the page down the middle and again and again, until he's torn it into strips. He balls the pieces and throws them at the typewriter keys. Then he pounds the table with his fist and barrels out the door.

Helene says, 'I think we should go after him,' but doesn't move.

'How about a cup of tea?'

She bites her lip. 'He needs support.'

'Don't look at me, I've done my time.'

She looks out the window. 'You mean you won't come with me?'

'*Go.*' I almost shout it.

She turns on her heel and runs out. I hear the slap of her feet on the boards and hear her calling, 'Sal, Sal!' The sound of his name hangs in the air. And all at once the house seems large and empty, cold. A cottage filled with moldy books, a grandfather clock that doesn't work, a broken rocker, faded curtains, stained walls. I back out the door abruptly, slamming into Margot on a deck rail, doing her eyes.

'Hey, watch it!' she calls out. 'You made me almost stab

myself. Everyone's in such a hurry, no one's looking where they're going – a girl could lose an eye or something.'

I sit next to her on the rail. 'Sal went off in a huff because he couldn't finish an article and Helene ran after him because . . . she just did.'

Margot bats her lashes at me. 'Don't you mind? I would. I mean, he was your boyfriend.'

'I'm trying not to, but I do. I do mind.'

'Why don't you just throw them out? It's your house.'

'But where would they go?'

'Who cares? They can figure that out.'

My feet jiggle on the rail. 'You're right, you're right, they have to go. I'll tell them first chance I get.'

'So you and me . . . we're staying?'

I look away, toward the sun, remembering the long, sleepy months I spent in Regency Hills, dulled by heat and drudgery and TV. The brown lawns and shadeless trees; the shallow end of an empty pool; a silent playground shimmering in August heat. 'I can't decide,' I tell her. 'Give me more time.'

She jumps off the rail and turns to go. I stop her, saying, 'Walk me to the store, I want to buy some things for supper,' and take her arm.

We walk together silently, her arm growing heavy in mine. Our pace slows until we're hardly moving at all. Then she whispers suddenly, 'There's something I want to tell you. Remember that time we walked on the beach and I told you how my mother comes to see me when she gets to the Coast?'

'Yes.'

'Well, I lied to you. She never visits and never writes. She could be dead for all I know.'

We move apart and quicken our step.

'I wanted you to know that. I don't want you thinking Bonnie would turn up and ruin things – you know, if we lived together. I thought if you knew that maybe you could make up your mind.'

My heart pings open then and I want to confess too. About the letters Bonnie sent when Margot was young, the notes I intercepted and hid. Three of them and a photograph of Bonnie with her face painted, lips pursed at the camera. She had meant well. Not meaning to hurt her daughter, hurting her anyway. As I did too.

But I don't tell her what I did. Because I couldn't bear it if she turned against me – not then and not now.

We turn onto The Boulevard, and Margot stops by the phone booth. 'I'm supposed to call Dad today, will you wait here? I won't be long.' She closes the door between us and I lean against it, facing the street.

I stand there watching passersby. Behind me Margot's voice rises. 'Sure I do,' she says, then, 'I do not!' The owner of the Mini-Mart rushes down The Boulevard. Wherever he's going I hope he'll be back in the store soon: I don't want to deal with his son.

Margot sticks her head out, 'He wants to speak to you too,' and we change places.

Jay gets right to the point. 'Well, I didn't expect her visit to turn into a permanent thing.'

'What did Margot tell you?'

'She says she wants to live with you – but I want her back home.'

'Only a couple of months ago you were begging me to look after her.'

'The situation's different now, I'm living alone.'

'You're lonely, is that it? You want Margot's company till you find another girlfriend.'

'I told Isadora to leave, we couldn't agree about Margot. Now there's no reason for her to live with you, she can come home.'

'If she wants to.'

A long pause. 'Anna, you can talk her out of this. Tell her how much I miss her, how you think she ought to live with me.'

'I don't know who she ought to live with, you or me. I know what Margot wants and what you want, now I have to think about what's right for me.'

'It's not your choice, you're not her legal guardian. I can force you to send her back. I'll come there and get her.'

'But you can't make her stay with you, she'll run away again, and the next time she might not come running to me.'

When he speaks again his voice is tight. 'I'm sure you'll make the right choice.'

'I'll let you know what I decide.'

On the street Margot asks, 'What did he say?'

'He said he'll respect my decision, whatever it is.'

She glances at me, looks away. 'I thought he'd go for the idea.'

The Boulevard is empty now. When we get to the Mini-Mart the store is deserted. Margot hurries up and down the aisles. 'No one here,' she says. 'Somebody's always here.'

'I saw the owner on the street.'

'Something's wrong, I know it.'

'Where's that boy, the owner's son?'

She backs up to the entrance, looks down The Boulevard and slaps a hand over her mouth.

'What is it? What's the matter?'

She runs off toward the beach. Slowly I follow her out the store and down the street. Ahead of me I see her like a ball spinning out of sight and imagine her bouncing down the landing, rolling to a stop in the sand. But I don't hurry up. I walk along as if nothing awaits me.

The sun is overhead and The Boulevard hot and still; my feet slip in my sandals. At the end of the street I stop and look down at the beach. A ring of people on the sand, a nervous crowd.

I walk to the edge of the group. All around me people are shifting, moving apart or closing ranks. From where I stand on tiptoe I can see something going on in center ring. Someone with light-colored hair is bent over a dark figure lying prone. I step deeper into the crowd.

Water drips from the long hair of the kneeling man. It drops onto the boy with his hands under his cheek and his face turned away from me. Neil rocks back and forth, pulling and releasing the sleeper's elbows. He has the other-worldly air of someone bowing and nodding in prayer. I picture him walking out of the sea with the clerk's body in his arms.

Someone says, 'It's no use,' and a wave of chatter rises. 'What'd he say?' 'He said –' 'What?' '*No use.*'

A boy who might've died in Nam drowned instead in a calm sea.

The crowd parts, or maybe I push my way through to get to the inner circle. The clerk lies across the sand, his body wrapped in wet fatigues, his face hidden. I don't want to see his face, too afraid of how it would look – spongy and blue, the eye sockets empty and smooth: my mother finally washed ashore.

When the owner of the Mini-Mart steps closer to the boy, the ring tightens. Neil gets up and stands over the dead clerk. People inch forward, I can hear their quick breathing, I can smell the old man's sweat. He kneels by his son's head. Don't touch him, I'm thinking. *Don't show his face.*

I spin around and shove back through the crowd. Margot appears from nowhere and grabs my arm, her voice wild: 'D'you see him there, dead like that? Even Neil can't do anything. He drowned himself – I should've known. I never should've left him alone!'

A small procession is forming. First the old man, then the drowned clerk, held up by two men, then a group moving in pairs. Margot pulls me into the line, but Neil stands apart. People race across the beach and onto The Boulevard; others line the street, standing in twos and threes, leaving a clear center path. Like guests at a wedding, watching us go by.

One of the bearers shakes his head and sweat runs from his forehead. Flies circle and swoop down: a lively buzz and slapping, buzz and smacking in succession. All this is somehow wrong. It seems to make the clerk deader than he is.

Behind me two women speak. 'He'll have to bury him on the mainland,' one says.

'He'd better call a water taxi.'

'A helicopter.'

'In this heat!'

By the time we get to the store the line has shrunk to eight – the owner, the bearers, Margot, myself and three more. We follow the old man into a back room of the Mini-Mart where the body is laid face up on a table. One of the bearers says he's going to get a doctor and call the police, then both of them walk out. The room is cool and stone-gray. The owner drags a chair to a place by his son's head and sits down. The rest of us hang back.

A woman says, 'We'll check on you later.'

Another says, 'You probably want to be alone right now.'

'Jack,' says the remaining man in the solemn way that men salute each other by their first names.

The man and two women leave, softly closing the back door. 'We should be going too,' I tell Margot.

Instead she walks up to the table and stares down at the clerk's face. 'Goodbye, Robert,' she whispers. I press against the back door, my hand on the knob. Suddenly Margot bends forward and kisses the dead boy's mouth.

I shut my eyes but keep seeing it – dead mouth, dead mouth. Lips cold with accusation, fat with rage. Blue with despair. A dead mouth calling my name. Mother speaks in a voice choked with water and pain: *Anna, come here.*

I shake my head.

Look at me.

No.

Kiss me.

No.

Stay.

'No!'

ELEVEN: 1974

I HAUL my duffel bag out of the closet and start to pack. Margot pokes her head in the room and says, 'What're you doing?'

'Can I talk to you a minute?'

'Sure.' She sits down next to me on the side of the bed.

'Remember when I talked to Jay that last time and you asked what he said? I didn't tell you everything. I didn't say that Isadora moved out, and how much he misses you.'

'He's on his own?'

'And wants you home.' I angle away from her on the bed. 'There's something else. I want to leave the island as soon as I can, and you've got to come along. You can't stay here alone. I think it's for the best if I put you on a plane, send you home and let you try to work things out with your dad. You're very special to him, you know.'

'*You're* very special to me.'

'I love you too,' I tell her, 'but it wouldn't work, I need space. I gave you a piece of my life – *two years* in Regency Hills. Now it's time to look after myself for a change. Just me. No one telling me how to live or holding me back.'

'I wouldn't crowd you. Ask Neil.'

'My mind's made up.'

She's still for a moment, then she gets up and backs away. 'Tell me something, why did Isadora go?'

'He told her to. Because of you.'

In the doorway she smiles. 'My father loves me too, you know.'

Later I head downstairs and sit down gingerly on the edge of the rocker.

'Go ahead and lean back,' Neil says from across the room. 'I fixed it.'

I look back at the long-broken rear leg, seeing a line of nail heads and traces of glue where once there was a deep crack. I slide back and begin to rock slowly, not trusting it yet.

'I'm leaving here,' I tell him.

'Soon?'

'Yes.'

He walks to the patio doors, his back to me. 'And Margot?'

'She can't stay without me.'

He opens the door and steps out. I watch from the chair as he starts doing tai chi, posing first on one leg, then the other, swinging his arms, but his balance is off. Neil stops and looks around. Fog has swept in and the sky, sea and sand are like a single length of cheesecloth. Suddenly he starts again, bend and twist, straighten and twist, all of it done too fast.

Margot comes up beside me, and I pull my eyes away from the deck. 'Still friends?' she wants to know. 'I mean, could I visit you sometime?'

I stop rocking. 'Still friends.' She turns my hand palm up, drops something into it and walks out.

The object feels good in my hand, dry, solid, smooth and cool: an oval stone with blue-white veins. Reminding me of something, the necklace Jay gave me once, that perfect shell on a long string. The one I wore the day I got lost in the fog, thinking it was a magic shell, that if I rubbed it and called his name he'd find me, only it didn't work.

Margot's stone is different, I can feel it pulsing in my hand. Absolutely magical. I put it in my back pocket and spring from the chair.

On The Boulevard, in the phone booth, I dial Jay. 'I'm calling to let you know what I decided,' I say. 'I'm sending her home.'

He lets out a breath. 'And you? What'll you do now?'

'Find a job, find an apartment. Same plan.'

'You won't stay in Onlyville?'

'I want to leave as fast as I can. I want to put the house on the market too, if that's okay. I can use the money, for one thing.'

'I always wanted you to sell.'

'There's an agent in the Cove I'll see, and leave with Margot after that. I'll drop her at the airport, you can meet her on the other end.'

'You'll let me know which flight?'

'Certainly.'

'Thanks,' he says. 'For everything.'

How long I've waited to hear that. How good it sounds.

❦

I walk to the Cove along the bay, past boats and cottages, a stretch of marsh, a point of land. Beyond that, a curved band of houses like beads on a string. I turn south to Bayside, stopping at the door to COVE REALTY.

The real estate office is jarringly modern with thin-slatted blinds and lacquered furniture. A red-headed woman motions me into a chair.

'I want to sell my cottage,' I say. 'In Onlyville.'

'A new house?'

'An older one.'

'In good shape?'

'Pretty good.'

She frowns slightly. 'Well, I'll have to look at it and see for myself. How much do you want for it?'

'I don't know.'

'Want to buy something else?'

'No.'

She flips through an appointment book and says, 'I can see it tomorrow afternoon.'

I give her the address. 'Do you think it'll take long to sell?'

'Depends on the house. Of course it's the wrong time of year – spring's my busy season – but we'll talk after I see the place.'

I shake her hand and walk out. Maybe tomorrow is too soon, the house isn't tidy yet. Maybe I can get a better price in the spring. Really, why do I have to sell at all, I can rent it out seasonally, and then if I want to come back . . .

You can always stay in another house.

You can always go to another place, somewhere you've never been before.

I cross the Handle and hike west by way of the sea. When I get to the abandoned house at the edge of town I stop and stare, waiting for its ancient ghosts to fly out and frighten me, as Jay always said they would. From behind the house comes Daddy instead, running out of my childhood. Daddy to the rescue again, his arms forever outstretched, eager to pull me back in time. I make him vanish with a blink. And when I walk by the house it winks at me glassy-eyed, its sagging porch a loose smile.

Ahead, the beach is deserted. I cross the sand, kick off my shoes and wade into the water. Daddy comes back again, blowing images into my eyes: carrying me beyond the breakers, stretching me across his arms, his voice low and reassuring. Daddy trying to teach me to swim.

Up, out, around, under, together, kick!

But I'm not doing it, can't do it – can't, can't! *I'm drowning!*

Back on shore, I bury my face in Mother's breasts and tell her that I almost drowned.

And one summer evening, under a hot purple sky, I stand in the surf and watch her swim away, away.

My mother drowned. Not me.

Her white-capped head like a ball blowing out to sea. *Floating, going under, gone. Away, away forever.*

And nothing I could have said or done would've brought her back.

All at once I tear off my clothes and toss them over my shoulder. I walk into the sea, and the water strokes my nakedness. Deeper still, I duck under a breaker and come up sputtering in the surf. I stretch my arms and kick my feet, slapping water back with my hands, snapping my legs open and shut, rising, falling, splashing forward, thrown back. And suddenly a wave lifts me – suddenly I'm buoyant! – and I flatten out and ride it in. Laughing with a mouthful of water, scrubbed on a washboard of sand, I lie on my belly, swept ashore, as the sea runs over me and slides back. It touches me; it lets go.

When I stand up and look down I see my reflection in a shallow pool. It grins back at me, gleaming.

❀

Helene and Sal are on the couch reading when I get back. I look around – something's changed – the typewriter's gone from the table. Alone, my Singer looks curious, out of place. When did I use it last? I carry it to a closet under the stairs and shove it way back, then do the same with a box of children's clothes in the kitchen all these months.

Something else is missing too – no, not a thing, a sound. My eyes shoot to the top of the fridge: the radio is turned off.

Quickly I cross the room and jump into the rocking chair, setting it in motion. 'Sorry to interrupt,' I say, 'but we have to talk.'

'Neil told us everything,' Sal says.

'About the boy,' whispers Helene.

'That's not what I want to talk about.'

They exchange glances. Helene reaches for his hand, then pulls back.

'I'm putting the cottage up for sale. I saw an agent this afternoon, she's coming here tomorrow. Then I'm going to finish packing, close the house and catch a ferry out of here. Margot's going home too, I'm taking her to the airport.'

They gawk at each other, then stare at me. 'But –' says Sal, and Helene raises a hand to her lips.

'This isn't much notice but it won't take you long to pack.'

'Where are we supposed to go?' Sal asks. 'I sublet my apartment till November.'

'I don't even *have* an apartment,' says Helene. 'And hardly any money left. I'll have to go on welfare – I'll have to live in a welfare hotel!'

I'm unmoved. 'Did you think you could live here forever? Did you think I'd support you when your money ran out?'

Helene's eyes are cloudy. 'I thought,' she begins. 'I didn't think . . . so soon.'

Sal turns to me, 'How much time do we have?'

'A day or two.'

'The house won't be sold right away. What's the rush?'

'Now that I've made up my mind to go I don't want to hang around. There's nothing for me here anymore.'

'But we don't have to go. We could stay till my apartment's free.'

'You and Helene?'

'We'll clean the place and close up when the time comes.'

'You and me?' Helene asks. 'Is that what you mean? The two of us?'

'We'll even pay you rent,' he says. 'A fair exchange. You need money, we need a place to live.'

I get up from the rocking chair and stand by a window. A breeze blows in, briny and sharp. I slam the window shut and spin around on my heel. *'Haven't I helped you two enough?'*

They inch closer on the couch and lock hands. I want to sink my teeth into their worried hands. *Are you worried about me?* I almost shout at them. *You have each other now but what about me? No!* and I can see them panic. *No, and you know why!* and I can watch them blush and squirm with guilt.

'One more time?' Sal asks.

'Please,' says Helene.

And finally I say yes, I'll let them stay, I need the cash. They say thanks and pay two month's rent in advance. They say, 'Let's have dinner at the Sea Breeze to celebrate,' and I agree. They're good enough to wait until I go outside before they embrace.

❀

I run to The Boulevard to phone Dad. 'It's me,' I say when he answers.

'Anna? Where are you calling from?'

'Onlyville.'

'You're still there?'

'Listen, Dad, I changed my mind. I've got some extra money now, so I thought I'd go straight to the city and not inconvenience you.'

'You're not coming? That's what you're saying?'

'I want to help you out but I think it's better to find an apartment right away.'

'Look at that,' he says. 'You want to help *me*. Wasn't I going to help you?'

'I guess we would've helped each other.'

'Now you sound like what's-her-name, my ex-friend. Always with the helping hand, the openness and honesty – so what does she do? She runs off without a word. Who knows where she went or who she's with, if she's all right. She could be dead!' Hard breathing in the wire.

'Dad?'

'I'm fine … just tired. Tired of so much worrying. And it's only going to get worse the older I get.'

'Dad, she's here, she's okay. In Onlyville.' Immediately I wish I hadn't said that.

'What? What did you say?'

'With me.'

'For how long?'

'All along.'

'And you didn't say a word about it? How could you not tell me? I could've gone and brought her home, and all this living by myself, this loneliness,' his voice rising, '*didn't have to happen*. It happened thanks to you and your damn jealousy! You always hated us together, didn't you?'

'Maybe I was being kind,' I say through my teeth. 'Maybe I was saving you the trouble of coming down here to find out she won't live with you again.'

'No!' he says. Then he sighs. 'Yes, I haven't been spending enough time with her, I work so hard, such long hours. Some women need attention, they need a lot of sweet-talk and evenings out. If that's what it takes, fine, I'll do it. I'll make time.'

'There's more to it than that,' I say.

'What do you mean?'

I take a breath – I don't have to say any more – but now there's no stopping me. 'She won't go back – not with you, not with me. She's staying here with Sal.'

'Who? Your boyfriend?'

'My ex –'

'You can't be serious. He's yours.'

'He *was*.'

'How can you let her do that? What's the matter with you!'

'She's free to do what she wants to. They both are.'

'I can't believe she'd do such a thing. I can't believe she'd turn around and take up with the first man she meets – Sal! *Your* man. You had something to do with this, didn't you? Did you leave them alone together? Did you send them for walks in the moonlight? Did you think about me for one second – *what it would do to me, what I was going through?*'

'You think I wanted it like this?' I yell at the phone. 'You think I'm glad they're getting it on? Do you know what it's like to see them together every day – what it's like for me? For *me*, I'm saying. *My* suffering, *my* pain. *What about me?*'

'You couldn't stop them?'
'NO, I COULDN'T STOP THEM!'
Silence. My ear is hot. I ask, 'Are you still there?'
'Sure, sure, I'm still here ... Okay, so I wasn't thinking – of course it's hard on you too. Sal's a bastard, no better than Helene. He doesn't deserve a girl like you. To hurt someone as sweet as you ... it hurts me too, what do you think? Sweet as honey, that's what you are, I always said.' He draws his breath in sharply: *'But how can you bear it?'*
'Dad?'
A short laugh. 'I was making a joke. Honey. Bear. Now you get it?'
'Honeybear?' The word sounding hollow and strange.
'That's what you are, my Honeybear.'
'Dad, I have to go now. I'll call you from the city.'

The sun is going down when we gather at the Sea Breeze, Helene, Sal, Margot and me, an empty chair saved for Neil. Behind the screened windows the bay glimmers purple and blue; boats are quickly turning black. When Neil comes in, Sal orders wine. When our glasses are raised up he says, 'To the future. Whatever it brings.'
'*Che sarà, sarà,*' says Helene. She sweeps her bangs aside and her forehead shows wide and smooth. 'I was thinking how much these past weeks in Onlyville have meant to me. For the first time in my life I feel *autonomous* – you know, in touch with who I am.' She smiles at Sal, bright-eyed, her lips moist. I've never seen her look more beautiful. 'I was reading that the more *self-actualized* a woman is the more she has to offer in a relationship. The better she can love someone else.'
'What will you do in the city?' I ask abruptly.
She glances at Sal again. 'The important thing is to find work that challenges you and makes you feel productive.'
'Sounds like all of us want the same thing,' I say, thinking, It'll be easier for them because they have each other. No, it'll be harder for them.
At some point during the meal Neil speaks up suddenly – 'I found a job' – and we put down our knives and forks. 'I'm going

to work in the store. Robert's old job.'

'You mean with Jack?'

'He can't manage by himself, not in the summer anyway. I can do other things when it's slow, carpentry and painting ...'

'You're staying here? Year-round?'

'But where will you live?'

'There's a room behind the store I can fix up.'

Exactly. Neil and Jack. Stay until you know what to do next. I nod at him, smiling, and he looks back at me steadily.

'That's what I ought to do,' says Sal, 'drop out, get back to the land, raise sheep or some damn thing. How about a commune in Onlyville? Sound good? What's the point of trying to make your name and trying to change the world? One man is nothing in the scheme of things. Neil's got the right idea.'

'Don't talk like that,' says Helene. 'Everyone's important. Anyway, I don't want to live on a farm, I want to work in the city.' She lights up a cigarette. 'I'd like to try interior design, I'd be good at that. I've decorated enough apartments in my time.'

Sal pays the bill, grumbling, 'Not as good as my food.'

'Where'd you learn to cook like that, anyway?' Helene asks. 'Your mother?'

'My mother was a lousy cook,' he says, 'you can't imagine.' I laugh out loud; I've heard it before.

We stand up and follow Neil and Margot onto The Boulevard, losing sight of them in the dark. Helene's cigarette darts to and fro as we walk along. 'What sort of work do you want to do?' she asks me.

'Anything I can get at first.'

'That's not much of a plan.'

'"One step at a time," my mother used to say. Right now that seems like good advice to me.'

She blows a pair of smoke rings and Sal breaks them with his hand. 'Dirty habit,' he says, and she flicks the cigarette off to the side. I quicken my step and walk on alone.

At the end of the street I find Margot on the landing, facing the beach, watching a pale figure gliding into the night. 'I'll miss him a lot,' she tells me. 'Not like missing Robert, not as quick as that. I'll miss Neil for a long time.'

And I feel it too, the urge to grab hold and hang on as you

watch someone leave, as you let him go. I sit down on a bench missing a center slat, feeling the space with my bottom as your tongue feels the hole in your gum after a tooth has been pulled out. Missing parts. If you're lucky you get used to it. One day you don't notice the emptiness in the same way – the gap has become part of what you are.

Margot sits next to me and hooks my arm. 'I'll miss you in a different way.'

'How?'

'In a happy way. Because I know we'll be in touch, I can call or visit you sometime. With Neil you don't know . . . maybe I'll never see him again.'

The night air is briny-damp. The surf booms, jarring the boards under our feet, and a dog races across the sand. Far away a ferry whistle hoots, then again and again. The last time clear and sweet, a cry of relief.

The realtor inspects the house and finds it to her liking. She even has a buyer in mind. We shake hands goodbye, then I go upstairs to finish packing. I'll be back for my sewing machine, back again when the house is sold – it's not like this is the last time I'm ever going to see the place. And yet.

Margot walks in – 'I'm ready' – a knapsack tied shut in her arms. She's wearing the same khaki pants and sweatshirt she arrived in. 'We can leave tonight, the last boat.'

I sit on the bed and run my hand over the sheet, absent-mindedly feeling for the imprint of Sal's body, despite his sleeping downstairs on the couch for weeks. 'Not tonight,' I say, though I can't give her a reason. 'Tomorrow.'

The morning air is sweet and fresh; the day will be sunny and warm. I kick off the sheet and lie still, letting a breeze brush over me. My body is heavy on the bed, making its own complaint about having to rise up, get ready and go.

I dress in jeans and a clean shirt, then drag my duffel bag into the hall and bounce it behind me down the stairs.

Helene and Sal look up from their coffee, heads together,

circled in steam, their hands sliding into their laps. In the steam floating over their cups I see a possible future I did not dare imagine before: me, alone in a small room, drinking coffee by myself.

Helene stands and takes my arm. 'Join us. I'll get you a cup.'

I sit on the edge of a chair, my duffel bag conspicuously at my side. She brings me a cup of coffee and I gulp it down. Sal asks, 'So what boat are you taking?'

'The ten o'clock.'

'We'll see you off.'

'Of course!' says Helene. She sits down beside me. 'Don't worry about the cottage. Sal and I . . . ,' then her voice fades.

Margot thuds downstairs in hiking boots, her knapsack hitched on her shoulder. She signals me with a nod and I get to my feet.

'Ready?'

'Ready.'

'Well,' says Sal.

'So!' says Helene.

We cross the boardwalks two by two, Margot and I up front, walking more quickly than we have to. The Boulevard is busy even at this hour, a blur of hats. Wagon wheels go clickety-clack.

Margot grabs my arm. 'Do you still have the rock?' she asks. 'You know, the one I gave you.'

I touch my back pocket, feeling a hard bulge: still there, that magic rock. 'Still here.' I poke the stone. Cool and inert to my finger, yet it jolts me like a live wire.

'Don't lose it,' she says.

'Never.'

At the end of the street Neil is leaning beside the door of the Mini-Mart, a white apron over his shirt. He waves us to a stop and hands Margot a bag of sandwiches. She throws an arm around his neck and whispers something in his ear.

'Take care of yourself,' I tell him.

He tucks his hands in his apron, then backs through the door.

Ahead the *Island Queen* is docking, butting and scraping the pier so that the boards rise, creaking, and flatten again. We move aside and watch a crush of passengers get off the boat. The ferry lightens, bobs up. Margot runs up the ramp and calls to us from the upper deck. I turn to Helene and we hug in such a way that only our shoulders meet. 'When you see your father,' she begins, then breaks off. She takes a breath and finishes: 'Tell him whatever you like.'

Sal and I shake hands. 'Good luck,' he says.

'You too.'

We wave at them from the top deck as the boat turns and pulls away, their figures shrinking on the pier until we hardly see them at all; until the island drops behind, a flat and hazy sandbar with no visible signs of life.

The wind is up, the sky clear. The boat dips and rises in a bright field of whitecaps. We leave the channel and pick up speed. The *Island Queen* sounds its whistle, long and trumpeting, and dances on the bay. In the distance I can see the mainland, thin and wide, opening between the water and the sky.

CYNTHIA HOLZ

Typeset in Trump Mediaeval,
printed and bound by The Porcupine's Quill, Inc.
The stock is acid-free Zephyr Antique Laid